## A gold medal dream come true...

This was Tuesday. Denny could make Mindy Blue taller, stronger, and more powerful in time for the tryout on Wednesday. And it wasn't just Mindy Blue that Denny's magic could rearrange. He could make me just a little bit taller, with the kind of legs top riders have: long, graceful, and muscular. And maybe make my eyes bluer and my hair blonder. If the magic was still around, that is. And if it was:

Was my life over? Or was it just beginning?

Don't miss Natalie and Denny
in the first Magical Mystery

# MY AUNT, THE MONSTER

or

# NEXT DOOR WITCH

third in the all-new Magical Mystery series!

"A delightful new series, with a pair of charming but flawed kids who act like real siblings, save that they keep stumbling into genuine magic . . . Seasoned with a hint of deeper mysticism, this is fine and lively writing that will appeal to any kid with a taste for the fantastic . . . I can't wait to see what else Mary Stanton has up her enchanted sleeve."
—Bruce Coville, author of *My Teacher's an Alien*

"Mary Stanton's Magical Mysteries are the stories that every child dreams of but rarely finds. Natalie and Denny have the style, pace and plots to push *Goosebumps* to the back of the rack."
—Charles Sheffield, creator of *Jupiter Line* Young Adult Science Fiction Novels

"The Magical Mysteries are funny, exciting adventures. Magic, science, horses, kids, other worlds—what more could anyone want, at any age?" —Nancy Kress, author of *Oaths and Miracles*

Books in the Magical Mystery Series

MY AUNT, THE MONSTER
WHITE MAGIC
NEXT DOOR WITCH

# WHITE

# Magic

## A Magical Mystery

★ ★ ★ ★ ★ ★ ★

# Mary Stanton

**B**

BERKLEY BOOKS, NEW YORK

WHITE MAGIC

A Berkley Book / published by arrangement with
the author

PRINTING HISTORY
Berkley edition / July 1997

The Putnam Berkley World Wide Web site address is
http://www.berkley.com

ISBN: 0-425-15904-3

BERKLEY®
Berkley Books are published by The Berkley Publishing Group,
200 Madison Avenue, New York, New York 10016.
BERKLEY and the "B" design
are trademarks belonging to Berkley Publishing Corporation.

PRINTED IN THE UNITED STATES OF AMERICA

10   9   8   7   6   5   4   3   2   1

FOR MADELINE AND THE TERRIFIC TRIO—
BIN, AMIR, AND MIKAAL

# ACKNOWLEDGMENTS

My thanks to Charles Sheffield, Ph.D., and Nancy Kress for the long weekend discussion that gave Natalie the key to the magic spell; to Sarah Higley, Nick DiChario, Dana Paxson, Duranna Durgin, and D. G. Smith; and to the librarians at the Walworth-Seeley Library.

# CHAPTER

# ONE

I WOKE UP FROM ONE OF THOSE SLEEPS WHERE YOU
are, like, practically drowned. My heart was thumping away. I was breathing hard. I'd been dreaming a
very weird dream. A nightmare, actually. My six-
year-old brother, Denny, had been in the middle of
this dream. I was awake now, but totally bizarre pictures still flew through my mind: Denny, green fire
flaming from his fingertips; Denny, a great glowing
pearl wrapped around his wrists; Denny, with his
red hair sticking up and his freckles washed out,
standing in front of a giant, ruby-eyed turtle.

Denny, doing magic.

Right. Like I was the sort of girl with a wizard for
a little brother. Fat chance.

I sat up, yawned big, and rubbed my face with both
hands. It was early, way early. My room was dark.
The curtains were open, and I could see the dawn
spreading around the trees. The moon was washed

and streaky, the color of a white T-shirt that'd been mixed up in a dark load of laundry.

I stopped rubbing my face and blinked. Trees? There weren't any trees in Manhattan, where I lived. The smells of summer came through the window screen: damp grass; the spicy-sweet scent of roses; the faint, totally neat odor of horse manure. There wasn't any horse manure in Manhattan, either—at least not near our apartment. So, I wasn't in Manhattan. I was at Uncle Bart's horse farm in upstate New York. That *had* been some nightmare to make me forget I was at Uncle Bart's.

I snuggled back down to go to sleep, just until the sun came up, which is when you start morning chores. On a horse farm, all the cool stuff happens at morning chores, like feeding and grooming and mucking out. This is when you get to know the horses in a personal way. Denny and I only get to spend a few months during the summer at Uncle Bart's stables. Every day I miss morning chores is a day I miss being with my favorite horse in the barn, Mindy Blue.

But I couldn't go back to sleep. There was a hummy noise around me, like an electric alarm clock before it goes off. The scary pictures of Denny stuck like Velcro to my brain. The hummy noise increased. Then my collarbone got hot—*really* hot. Something around my neck was practically burning me up. I flattened my hand over the top of my pajamas. There *was* something burning me! I jumped out of bed with a yell, smacking at it. Whatever it was, it was small and round, and when I smacked it, it cooled down fast, like shutting off a burner on a stove. I pulled my chin in and tried to look straight down at what my hand covered. A creamy pearllike light shone under my palm. Bits of green mist curled around my thumb. I'd seen that color green before. In my nightmare. The nightmare about Denny, the wizard. I peeled my hand back, inch by inch.

There it was. My pearl necklace. The one I'd gotten months ago, the day I turned thirteen. The necklace I'd dreamed about, just now. In my nightmare, Denny had used the pearl to start the magic.

The necklace felt warm and smooth. About as unmagical as a necklace can be. I took it off, held it up and swung it back and forth in the dawn light creeping in through the window. The pearl was creamycolored, like Dad's morning coffee. Little flashes of green magic floated off the surface. The chain was gold and so was the setting that held the pearl. I stopped swinging it and brought the pearl closer to my face. There was something weird about the setting. "What the heck?" I said out loud.

I remembered the day I got this necklace as clear as clear. It was the last day I was twelve. Dad and Mom made this big deal about giving me the present at breakfast, saying how I was now a teenager and this was a present that would mark my entry into a new phase of life, blah-blah-blah and all that. So I was excited even before I opened it. I remembered those strong feelings even now: I'd torn off the gold foil paper, opened the magical box, and seen the pearl shining there, like a tiny moon in a red velvet sky.

"The setting is a rose, your birthday flower," Mom had said.

I remembered that all right, the gold rose with its fragile petals clasping the pearl. Only the setting wasn't a gold rose anymore. It was a turtle. A turtle with teeny ruby eyes. It was the Great Turtle that guarded the Jewel at the Heart of the World.

*How did I know that?*

I'd seen Denny in front of that turtle in my nightmare.

I sat up with a gasp. My brain was going a hundred miles a minute.

Denny and the green fire.

The turtle.

The nightmare was all true!

I mean, I'd dreamed about Denny as a wizard, but I hadn't dreamed what had happened the day before. Denny had turned his parakeet, my cat, Bunkie, and my aunt Matty into a griffin. A griffin is a supposedly mythical monster with the head of an eagle, the body of a dragon, and the claws of a lion. It is also a very bad-tempered sort of monster, and Denny and I'd had some job unmagicking it back into his bird, my cat, and my dragonish aunt Matty before Mom and Dad found out about it. I'd worked so hard to get rid of that spell that I hadn't even thought about what was going to happen after the crisis was over.

Well, the crisis was over. But the pearl necklace was telling me that the magic was still here. And that Denny was in the middle of it.

I got back into bed, stiff as a board and twice as scared.

What kind of messy magic was Denny going to do today?

# CHAPTER

## two

MY GOOD OLD CAT BUNKIE PRANCED DOWN THE BED-spread and I woke up again. By the way the sun was slanting on the worn-out old carpet in the second-best bedroom, it was way late in the morning. Maybe even close to lunch. I couldn't believe I'd slept so long after waking up at the crack of dawn and realizing my brother was a wizard. Total fear must, like, poop you out.

I tried to give Bunkie a good-morning pat, but she wriggled around and growled. Her tail lashed back and forth. This is how a cat shows it's mad at you. Bunkie had *no* reason to be mad at me. Except one: she was mad about the time she'd spent as the lion part of a griffin. And my brother the wizard had done it.

A six-year-old wizard! What a disaster this was going to be. Denny looks just like your ordinary six-year-old. He's got a lot of freckles. Red hair that sticks up unless I comb it down with water every morning. He likes snakes, gross food, and Spiderman. He hates baths, girls, and vegetables. He's your average six-year-old—which is, like, your basic demon in a boy suit.

I'd learned all about Denny's magic when I was working to get that spell fixed. The magic took things apart and put them together again in different ways. Pictures flew through my mind of Denny loose upon the world with his magic: the school van turned into a giant video game. The Empire State Building into a mass of Tinkertoys. Denny's magic gave him power!

Jeez!

Up until Denny got this magic, my life had been way cool. Back in Manhattan, Mom and Dad own this advertising agency. We live in a three-bedroom condo on the fortieth floor of a big building on West Seventieth Street. I have my best friends at school and this really neat sort of boyfriend named Brian Kurlander. I'm in an after-school band that's like fantastic. We call ourselves the Awesome Attitudes. Except for geography, I even like all my seventh-grade classes. Up until now there were only a couple of things I'd wanted different about me and my life. I mean, I really wish Mom and Dad would let me wear just a little bit of makeup. And it'd be great if my eyes were bluer and my hair was blonder. But that's small stuff—not a problem.

Not nearly the problem a person has who is faced with a wizard in the family. And Denny was the kind of little brother that just, like, bugged the life out of a person, for no reason. I mean—look at what he'd done to my cat! My life was changed forever. No doubt about it. I could just see it: Denny turning my bedroom curtains into a prom dress; or my prom dress into curtains. I mean, forget the usual stuff like Denny turning healthy vegetables into Rice Krispie treats. You could even forget the Empire State Building and the school van. Denny would use his magic to drive me bughouse bananas and get me into trouble.

Those pictures in my head got wilder and wilder. Denny turning my horse Mindy Blue an actual blue color. Denny turning me into a lobster if I didn't let him play his kazoo with the guys in Awesome Attitude . . . Denny as king of the world, with *me* as the bozo!

*Aaaaggghhh!*

I flopped back onto the pillows. Oh, no! The world and all my friends would be in total terror of my baby brother! I pulled the covers up over my head. It was nice and dark under there. "Now, Natalie," I told myself. "Denny's basically a good kid. Basically."

Bunkie patted my face through the quilt. I uncovered myself, sat up, and went, "Hey, Bunk," in this feeb voice. She stalked down the bedspread and sat down on my chest. Her big yellowy eyes looked into mine. She squeezed them shut then opened them again. "Bunkie, what am I going to do?"

She purred. It was *not* cool to get this hysterical. There had to be some good to this mess. Maybe Denny's being a wizard wouldn't make my future as horrible as I thought. Maybe it'd be like, an advantage.

Well, yeah! He could rearrange the shape of anything at all, couldn't he? There had been one special thing I'd dreamed of for years and years. Maybe Denny's magic could help me and my horse Mindy Blue do it.

I wanted to ride in the Olympic equestrian team!

I got breathless just thinking about it. Horses that can qualify for the Olympic equestrian team cost tens of thousands of dollars. There was no way Mom and Dad could afford to buy me a horse like that. And Mindy Blue, as much as I loved her, wasn't big enough, or strong enough, or trained enough in the right way to be an Olympic star. But Denny's magic could rearrange the shape of anything at all, couldn't it? He could rearrange Mindy Blue into a champion!

"Could that really happen, Bunk?" It seemed way, way too good to be true. Like waking up and suddenly finding out you were richer than anybody.

There had to be a catch to this. Maybe the magic hurt the animals and people. I mean—you just never know about that sort of thing until you test it. I'd die before I'd let anything hurt Mindy Blue.

Bunkie'd been one third of a griffin and it hadn't hurt her, had it? I petted Bunkie. She purred. She rolled over on the bedspread and yawned, thumped her tail a couple of times, and squeezed her eyes closed. This was regular cat-stuff, which she'd done a lot before she'd been turned into the lion part of the griffin. I tried to think of what a cat would react to, to see if she was still normal inside of herself.

"Would you like some kitty kibbles?" I asked her. This was her favorite breakfast.

"Meeow!" she said. She sat up fast, then pounced on my hand under the bedspread. I wiggled my fingers. She bit at them and rolled over and over. This was normal. I tried it the other way, just to be sure.

"Sorry, Bunk, but we're totally out of kitty kibbles. I gave them all away. To Brandy the dog." She growled. Uncle Bart's golden retriever Brandy was Bunk's worst enemy. So she was okay, mentally at least. And she obviously had the same color fur and normal amount of legs and ears that'd she'd had before the griffin adventure. So maybe Denny could do it, if I asked him nicely. Maybe he could transform me and Mindy Blue into champions.

"This could be way cool, Bunk."

She flattened her ears and growled. She only did that when she didn't like something. And I knew she liked me. Unless the magic *had* changed her inside, after all.

"Finally!" hollered Denny. He stood at the door. So *that* was why she growled. I'll bet she was holding a grudge against my brother the wizard. I felt like growling myself. Bunkie jumped to the floor and scooted under my bed. I pulled the covers up to my chin and peered at Denny.

Did he look . . . different?

He walked smack into my room without permission, as usual. Did he think he could barge right in just because he was a wizard? Nah, Denny's always had nerve. It's very normal for him to drive me nuts. But didn't he look—sort of crazed?

I watched him carefully. If he moved away from the door, I could grab Bunkie and be out of there before he could turn me or my cat into Tinkertoys.

He marched right up to the bed. I shrank down under the cover. He had bits of hay in his red hair. "I thought you were going to sleep all day."

This was normal. I decided to be normal back. "Shut up, Denny," I said. "And beat it. You're scaring my cat. She's probably never going to come near you again after you turned her into a grif—" I stuffed the blanket in my mouth to shut myself up. I'd forgotten that Mom and Dad were still here. For all I knew they were lurking just outside my bedroom door. "Where are Mom and Dad?" I whispered. "I thought they were off to Paris this morning."

Denny hopped on one leg over to the window. "They left already. Mom came in here to say good-bye and she said you were too pooped out to wake up."

"Did they, you know, say anything?"

" 'Listen to Uncle Bart. Don't run off from Althea. Eat vegetables and no more than six Oreo cookies a day.' "

"You know you've got a two-cookie limit," I said. "And I don't mean that, I mean about—you know. About the magic."

"What?"

Hmm. I sat up, cautious-like. It didn't look like Denny was going to pull anything funny—at least not right away. "What do you mean, 'what?' You know very well what I'm talking about."

Denny bugged his eyes out at me, stuck out his

tongue, and went "Yeeeeecch." I shivered. I couldn't
think of anything worse in this life than a bratty wizard. But it's best, they say, to show no fear. I put my
voice real low, in case anyone else was around to
hear. "I mean, did they say anything about you being
a wizard?"

Denny looked puzzled, and said, "Huh?"

Well, this was just great. Denny didn't seem to remember a thing. I wound some of my hair around my
finger and tugged on it. I had to think. In the mean-
time Denny hopped all around the room on two feet,
this time. It made very loud thumps. "Uncle Bart
wants to know aren't you ever going to get up and do
your barn chores and make me some lunch?"

This is just like Denny, to make it out that Uncle
Bart was mad at me. I knew he wasn't. Uncle Bart
was totally laid-back. This is one of the reasons
Denny and I like to stay with him when Mom and
Dad have to go off on business trips. "I'm not getting
up with me in my pajamas and you standing there,
bozo. Go away!"

He stopped thumping, stuck his forefingers into
the corners of his mouth, and made a noise like
*gaaack!* I started to pitch a pillow at him and stopped
just in time. Getting a bratty old wizard aggravated
at you wasn't such a good idea. If he still *was* a wizard. I changed my mind about wanting him to beat
it. There were some important things I had to ask
him. "C'mere."

He stuck his lower lip out. Denny's as stubborn as
a fire hydrant: you can whack him all you want and
he won't move. It is very annoying. I patted the bed-

spread. "Sit down, Denny. I just want to ask you something."

"What?"

"Sit down and I'll tell you."

He sat down like the mattress was boiling hot. Bunkie poked her head out from underneath the bed and hissed at him. Bunkie likes Denny, goodness knows why. If she was hissing at him, maybe she was sniffing the magic. I began to wish I hadn't made him sit on my bed. I began to wish he was sitting somewhere else. Like Tokyo. Then I thought about the Olympic equestrian team. About the gold medal that would be mine if Denny could magic me into a star rider.

*Without working at it?* A voice inside me asked. *Without earning it?* "I could never do it myself," I said out loud. "And it'd wouldn't really hurt anybody, would it?"

"Huh?" said Denny.

I looked at him. Three feet four inches high, and filled with awesome power. And he didn't even know it.

*Maybe,* that voice inside my head whispered, *maybe* you're *the one with the magic. After all, who has the pearl necklace? The key to the magic?*

I patted my pajama top. The necklace was still there. Was I the one who was the wizard? Did I *want* to be the one who was the wizard?

I was so mixed up I didn't know *what* I wanted. Except one thing: I wanted to see some more magic. Right now. Just to know I wasn't crazy.

I wound my hair tighter around my finger. Maybe

he'd remember if I prodded him some. I tried to decide where to start without scaring him. "How's T.E. this morning?" I asked, casual like.

He looked surprised at my question about his parakeet. "T.E.'s okay." Then he squinted at me, which meant he was suspicious. "Why do you care?"

"I just thought he might be tired or something. You know, after all that time he spent being a monster. Pretty exhausting, I'd guess."

"You're crazy," Denny said flatly. He jumped off the bed and headed toward the door. Just in time I grabbed his jeans by one of the loops in back and hung on. He wriggled like a fish on a hook, with no noise but a lot of determination.

"Where do you think you're going?"

"There's a riding class this morning, in the big arena. It's to get Uncle Bart's students ready for the Olympic stuff. I'm gonna ride Susie in it. Leg-*go*!"

I didn't let go. I held on. My breath was going faster and faster. The qualifying trials for the Olympics! The absolute dream of my life!

This was Tuesday. Denny could make Mindy taller, stronger, and more powerful in time for the tryout on Wednesday. Riders who qualified in the trials had a real chance at winning a spot on the Olympic equestrian team. And it wasn't just Mindy Blue that Denny's magic could rearrange. He could make me just a little bit taller, with the kind of legs top riders have: long, graceful, and muscular. And maybe make my eyes bluer and my hair blonder. If the magic was still around, that is. And if it was:

Was my life over? Or was it just beginning?

# CHAPTER

## three

WELL, I BLABBERED ON AND ON TO DENNY UNTIL I was totally pooped out about the green fire and the Great Turtle who was there in the magic. Denny *still* didn't remember he was a wizard.

So? Maybe he wasn't. At least, not anymore.

Was this magic thing just a . . . a . . . there was a word Dad had for this: was it an *aberration*? If this whole thing magic thing was an aberration—which means, Dad says, temporarily going off the normal way of doing things—then maybe Denny had finished with being an aberration and was now a normal kid. I hung on to Denny's jeans and thought about this. My arm was getting a cramp in it, so I had to think fast. If Denny's magic was an aberration and he couldn't do it anymore, that was one thing. Or maybe he didn't want me to know he could do magic. That was something else again.

This idea that maybe Denny didn't trust me

enough to share the magic was incredibly gruesome. He trusted me, didn't he? I mean, we'd been through all kinds of stuff together. Some kind of very strange thought hit me then: the magic didn't harm Bunkie. She was the same good old cat she'd always been. But did it change the people who *used* it? Did it make them sneaky and suspicious?

*So what if it did?* that little voice whispered.

I thought about the Olympics, one year from now. In my mind I heard: *And for the Gold Medal for the U.S.A.—NATALIE ROSS on MINDY BLUE!* How could making that happen change Denny into a sneaky little person who wouldn't tell me a thing?

*Because it's power,* that little voice in my head said. *And power can be a dangerous thing.*

I could handle power. I knew I could. I could be a star, if Denny would just shape up and give me a hand. And he could give himself a hand, too. He could fix his pony Susie up so that she'd be a winner. Except not as much of a winner as Mindy Blue and I would be. I could, like, point this out to him.

"The show is for professional riders only, Denny. The ones who are trying to get picked for the Olympic equestrian team. You have to have scored a whole pile of riding points just to register. There's no way you and that Shetland pony are going to get into those jumping classes." I grabbed his middle with both hands and turned him around to look at me. "Except one. You could do it with magic."

Denny's blue eyes bored straight into mine. "I don't know what you're talking about. And you let me go!" He took a huge breath and then hollered,

"Yaaaaahhh!"—which was sure to bring Uncle Bart or Althea, our tutor, or *somebody* at a run.

"Be quiet a second!" I stuck my hand over his mouth—which made the *yaaahh* more of *yurk!*—and said in this low fierce way, "You *can't* have forgotten about the green fire? And most of all, Denny, the turtle?"

That got him. For a second, just a second, the word 'turtle' made a little green flash in his eyes. But the flash wasn't more than a second. Then it was gone. I mean, the turtle was awesome; not the kind of reptile a person was likely to forget. The turtle was the Source of the Magic. The turtle was, like, an emperor. I was so bummed I shook Denny. He squealed, like he does when something *really* hurts. Tears started up in his eyes. I let Denny go. I couldn't believe I was hassling him. "I'm sorry, Denny." I hugged him. Then I kissed his cheek. He tasted like sweat and grime. I was suddenly so ashamed I wanted to crawl under the bed with Bunkie. The magic changed people all right. Look how it was changing me. I was turning into the creep of the universe.

"I don't know what magic you're talking about!" he said again. "You're just stupid."

Normally this would start one of those conversations like, "who's stupid?" "you're stupid," and like that, but I felt so bad, I just nodded. It was clear as water that I'd let *greed* get in my face, big time. Ugh.

"So you know you're stupid," said Denny, grinning.

"I know I'm stupid."

"How stupid are you? Are you as stupid as . . ." He

blabbered and blabbered. Was I as stupid as a worm?
As stupid as a clam? As stupid as dog doo? I didn't
say a word back. I was so embarrassed about getting
greedy over the magic, I could have taken a lot more.
After a while, though, I got sick of it. I was sorry, but
it was too much to ask me to grovel. Dad says
"grovel" means to, like, crawl and be sorry. Denny
went on and it didn't look like he was going to quit
until I did some groveling. So I shrieked, "Shut up,
Denny!" I mean there is a limit to how much a person
can take. He stuck out his tongue. We glared at each
other.

"You're still in *bed,* Natalie?"

Well, this was totally terrific. There she was at my
bedroom door. Aunt Matty herself. One third—the
dragon third—of the griffin that Denny couldn't remember unmagicking. Big as life and twice as cross.

She marched right into my room. "Do you know
what time it is? And I heard you yelling at Denny.
For heaven's sake, you are certainly old enough to
treat your little brother with some respect."

"Yeah!" Denny grinned all over his freckled little
face.

"You will apologize."

"Hoo!" Denny laughed.

"Well, Natalie?" my aunt asked in a cold way.
"We're waiting."

"Yeah!" Denny chortled. "We're waiting!"

One look at Aunt Matty waiting for me to grovel
to my little brother told me that she didn't remember
any more about the magic than Denny did. She
would have been a lot more respectful of him herself

if she had. I couldn't believe it. What good was the magic if you forgot it was there?

Except *I* knew it was there.

I grabbed at my neck. There was the necklace, tucked safely under my pajama top. The pearl warmly buzzed in my hand, like a nice little bee. The magic wasn't an aberration. I knew it. I knew there was magic there as sure as my name was Natalie Ross. Maybe I could figure out how to use it myself.

Of course!

I sat there with my mouth half-open. Me! Natalie Ross the wizard. Why the heck didn't I think of that before? I didn't have to be mean to my little brother. I could do it myself! "Hooray!" I shouted. Then: "Beat it, Denny!" I jumped out of bed.

Aunt Matty gave me the Look. A sort of what-kind-of-dog's-dinner-are-you-today look. I didn't even care. I was too busy whacking myself, like, mentally. How could I be so dumb? I'd almost blown it! I'd almost given the magic to Denny by asking him all those questions.

"Natalie? That's all you've got to say? 'Beat it'? What a *marvelous* apology."

I didn't even care that she was, like, sarcastic. I just wanted to be alone with the necklace. So I said, nice as pie, "Sure, Aunt Matty." I wasn't mad at Denny, either. I said I was sorry, again, as nice as I could make it. Then Bunkie came out from under the bed and growled at either Aunt Matty or Denny or maybe both. This started a wrangle. Aunt Matty threw up her hands and yelled, "Stop!"

We stopped. She gave a big huge sigh and mut-

tered "aaaggh" and "you're shortening my *life*!" and
stuff like that. Then: "It's past time to get up,
Natalie." Like I didn't know I was still in my pajamas
at ten o'clock in the morning? "Bart could use a hand
in the barn. He's got quite a few students coming in
for this class this morning. He's schooling his top students for the equestrian team. And you know how
important the Olympic trials are for him and the
farm. I'd help him myself, but I'm off to Chicago for
a meeting."

"Right, Aunt Matty."

"And it does *not* do to be lazing about even when
there is no work to be done. It's not healthful."

"No, Aunt Matty."

She gave me a beady look from her sharp black
eyes. "Well? I'm waiting."

Jeez! "I'll get right there, Aunt Matty. Just give
me a second to get dressed."

Well, you would have thought that would get Aunt
Matty out of my room, but no such luck. Neither of
them looked like they were going to leave anytime
soon; Denny because he spends most of his time following me around and making me crazy, and Aunt
Matty because she's so darn bossy she wanted to
make sure I was following orders. Before I had time
to think of some way to get them nicely out of the
way, Brandy the dog raced into the room, her tail
wagging. She screeched to a halt when she saw Bunkie. Bunkie dived back under the bed. Brandy dived
under the bed after Bunk. I dived after Bunk. Denny
grabbed Brandy by the tail. A whole entire golden
retriever being held by the tail under your bed gets

pretty bumpy. There was a rumpus. Aunt Matty rapped the wall with her sharp knuckles and hollered, "Order!"

"Natalie, you not up yet?" A tall slim girl in jeans and a flannel shirt walked in. A dog leash dangled from one hand. Brandy cocked one brown eye at her and grinned. She flattened herself on the floor and wagged her tail. "Oh, darn! You caught me!" that tail said.

I couldn't believe it. Now Althea Brinker was in my room! If this kept up, I wouldn't be surprised if Mindy Blue herself walked in, along with Susie the Shetland, Uncle Bart, and all three New York State football teams.

Actually, Althea is pretty cool and I didn't mind her in my room at all. I didn't think she was so cool when I first met her. She is the tutor that Mom and Dad hired to make sure that Denny and I don't lose all of our brains when we have to be out of school. She's got red curly hair and these really slick glasses. And although she's kind of pale from all this studying she does as a graduate student, she's definitely not a dork. She's like super excellent.

Althea showed some of that super excellence in getting all those people and animals out of my room. She made Brandy sit. She pried Bunkie off the curtains where she was hanging by her front claws and handed her to me. She brushed Denny's hair flat with her hand and made him stop saying "get Bunkie, Brandy."

"Kind of crowded in here," Althea said. There was a little smile around her mouth. "I'll bet if we got out of here, Ms. Carmichael, we could give Natalie a chance to get up and dressed."

This was the best idea I'd heard all morning. I mean, what did these people think—that my room was a subway station?

Althea gave me sort of a secret wink, then held the bedroom door wide open. Denny skipped out like one of the villains in his Spiderman comics was after him, Brandy at his heels. Aunt Matty sort of sniffed, then marched out the door. Even Bunkie squirted out, her tail waving like a furry gray flag.

Althea gave me the okay sign and sat down in the chair next to the little desk. "I can't wait for you to come out and see the training sessions this morning. Your uncle says there's one rider that absolutely terrific. You should see her school her horse. He's a white stallion, one of the most magnificent horses I've ever seen in my life."

I could just imagine it. Tall and strong. With the fabulous muscular hindquarters and the chest of a champion. If I could just figure out how to use the magic, I could do that for Mindy Blue.

"Bart thinks the rider might have a spot on the Olympic team if she can get the financing. He's really anxious to have her do well at the qualifying trials."

I felt a frown on my face. *I* was going to be at the qualifying trials. That is, if people would just leave me alone so that I could figure out the magic.

"You'll like her, I think, Natalie. I do already. And you should see her ride! Her name's Amanda. She's been a working student's of Bart's all winter long. I guess she was just terrific help in the barn. Bart said she worked like a dog. She hauled manure through snowstorms to be able to afford to live here with Bart. She rode every day, in the worst kind of weather. All of that for this wonderful horse. Her folks don't have a lot of money. But, boy, does she have talent!"

I had to see this wonderful stallion and Amanda the star rider. With a little bit of luck, Althea would be talking about me like that—very soon! I gave a little smile.

Althea tilted her head at me and looked puzzled. "Did you—um—get up on the wrong side of the bed this morning? You're not at all like yourself, Natalie." She leaned over and tucked my hair back behind my ear. "You seem—different. You're not jealous of Amanda, are you? She's got some pretty stiff competition ahead of her. I'd like you two to be friends."

Jealous? Amanda should be the one to be jealous!

Just then I caught sight of myself in the bureau mirror. I had a horrible scowl on my face. Althea was right. I didn't feel like myself, that was for sure. I felt . . . cross. Weird. I pushed away the sneaky thought that the magic might be dangerous to me in a very strange way. I had to try it. I had to. I didn't want to think about whether I should keep on being Natalie Ross, Very Obedient Thirteen-Year-Old. I wanted to become Natalie Ross, Gold Medalist and Star Magician. "I'll be down in a minute. I've just got a few things to do."

Althea stood up. "Right. Look, I'll see you in the barn pretty quickly? There's a lot to do today."

"Sure."

Althea closed the door softly behind her. Finally! I was alone. Alone with the pearl necklace.

I SLIPPED THE PEARL NECKLACE OVER MY HEAD AND grasped it in the palm of my hand. It was mine. All mine. And I was the only one who knew what it could do.

But how did the magic start? I held the necklace before my eyes. If I called to the turtle, would the magic come to me? "Oh, turtle," I whispered.

No answer. Rats. How could I become Natalie Ross, star rider, if the darn turtle didn't show when it was called? I called the turtle again, and again. When nothing happened, I began to feel like the biggest bozo in the seventh grade of the universe. What magic? I wasn't crazy. I knew I hadn't imagined the griffin—had I? The pearl had wakened me early this morning just filled with magic—hadn't it?

I got mad, I admit it. Once in a while, Mom says, everyone gets mad. It's normal. But this was a *big* mad. The kind of mad where you feel there's something huge outside of you, making you madder and madder. The anger felt like it was outside of me. It was so much outside of me that it felt . . . real. I got so mad I threw the necklace away from me.

The gold chain caught on my wrist. The pearl settled into the palm of my hand. It started that humming that'd wakened me before dawn. Something was happening! Finally!

The sunlight in my bedroom dimmed, as if a giant wing swept over the sun. There was something in the room with me. A huge thing practically breathing down my neck.

I stopped being mad. I started getting scared.

The gold chain tightened around my wrist like the string on a gigundous kite. The pearl grew bigger and bigger, like a rising moon. It spread quietly, steadily, like a balloon getting pumped up with gas. It grew so big it filled the room, from wall to wall, from ceiling to floor. The silky sides pushed against my whole body. I pushed my nose against the silk and looked and looked. The light inside shone creamy clear. Two ruby-rose points glowed in the middle. It was the turtle. Huge. Astonishing. And kind. The whole front of me felt warm and safe.

But my back and neck were cold.

With me, in my room, dimming the sunlight like a huge ugly bird, was Something. Big. Deep. Angry.

I shivered, afraid to turn around. Behind me was this hateful thing. A shadowy presence that threatened something awful. That hissed words at me I could barely hear. I strained my ears. I listened as hard as I could.

*Denny*. The cold thing said: *Denny. Denny-denny-denny-denny*. And there was hunger in its voice.

"No!" I screamed. I struggled to turn around and face it. It was hard. Like pulling on a pair of wet jeans. But I did it. I turned around, my back to the pearl and all it promised. A foul brown mist filled my bedroom. There was a winged black shape in the middle. No face, no eyes. Just inky shadow. It was horrible, hearing my brother's name in that awful icy whisper, coming from that no-face shape. "You stop!" I screamed to that black nothingness, "You shut up!"

But the hateful chant went on.

The pearl was warm behind me. It bumped gently against my back. I was holding the gold chain so hard my hand hurt. The turtle was in there—I knew. I knew it the way you know that music is beautiful, without thoughts, just feelings. "Oh, sir," I whispered to the turtle, "Oh, sir. Help."

The pearl pulsed with huge—but gentle—thumps. Like a soothing sort of heart beat. There was a hum, like a thousand stars chiming all at once. The brown-black shade over the sun whisked away. The sunlight in my room burst bright. I tumbled backward, into the pearl, in the silky light, the turtle above me with its great glowing eyes.

It felt so sweet, so soft to be there. Like flannel sheets that have been washed about a zillion times and smell of spring. Like a pool of water so warm you couldn't tell your skin from it, water so safe you could breathe it. I held on to the gold chain and floated, for how long, I didn't know. I forgot about the dark wing over the sun, the deep angry presence outside. The beast.

As I floated I saw the things of the world and how they were made. Cars and people and mountains and rivers. Food and plants and dishes and chairs. Jeans and T-shirts and airplanes. All made of zillions and zillions of little whirling worlds. Little specks of stuff.

The stuff was . . . "Molecules!" I shouted. Molecules were the things Denny could take apart to do his magic.

I mean, molecules were so *cool*. Althea had made Denny and me memorize about molecules—the smallest physical unit of a compound element. And each of these molecules, in the cars and the plants and the animals, had the silvery specks of atoms whirling around in them like a carousel at a circus. As I floated there in the heart of the pearl, I whispered, "Where is this?"

*you are in the Jewel at the Heart of the World*, the mighty turtle breathed.

The source of the magic! It felt wonderful, being in the jewel. I thought about molecules and how Denny could take them apart and move them around to make new things. He could push them around, to make time go backward or forward. Or even stop the molecules from spinning and make time stop.

"How?" I asked, looking up. "How do I make the magic work?"

The voice of the turtle came from everywhere around me.

*together,* It said in a rumbling whisper, *not alone.*

"With Denny?" I asked as I floated there, then added, "sir," because this turtle was the sort of reptile a person had to respect.

*with Denny*.

"Excuse me, but I don't think Denny's all that hot on the magic, sir. I mean, why does he have to even—"

The pearl sea surged. I rose up, plunged down. Yikes! There was the faintest rumble, then a very firm *no*.

"No" what? "No" I couldn't have the magic myself?

*together*, the turtle said, reading my thoughts.

I couldn't do the magic alone? I had to have Denny? I wanted to cry.

Then:

*watch this, my dearest dear. your task is to guard the jewel within.* A girl came into the pearl, as if she had stepped through a mirror. She swam through the milky waters, astride a silver horse. She glistened like precious ebony. The horse spun in graceful curves, flew high, swept low. I was shy with the beauty of it.

As I floated there, watching, wondering, the black shadow came back! Outside the pearl, it shadowed the pearl sky, once with its dirty light, twice with its mudlike light, and then . . .

"The beast!" I cried. A cold current brushed through the sea, like a thin hair in a braid. "The beast with wings!" I said.

The silvery horse and the ebony girl looked up. She screamed! And I screamed, too. "Get away from her!" I shouted.

*be gone!* the turtle commanded.

The shadow flipped away, a shark turning away in the water.

She was safe! The bright stallion dipped and flew. I shouted "hooray!" and "hooray" again!

And then the turtle sang. A song I didn't know. A melody I would never forget. A song with words I couldn't make out. I strained my ears to hear it. The turtle's voice was so big, so majestic! Like the grandest trumpet in the most magnificent parade a person could imagine. I moved my arms like a bird flying, to swim through the warmth and reach him and that wonderful song. I pushed against the soft side of the pearl with my feet and tried to fly . . .

. . . and thumped down on the floor of my bedroom, the necklace dangling from my fingers.

It took me a few seconds to get my head on straight. I mean, to go from swimming around in this great pearl sea, seeing the jewellike rider and her horse—and most of all, hearing that song—and then to get whomped back into Uncle Bart's second-best guest bedroom with its worn-out rug and beat-up furniture was quite a surprise.

I blinked, took a couple of deep breaths. I clutched the necklace in my hand. It crackled a little.

Crackled?

I opened my fist. There was a bit of shimmery paper—like tissue paper—wrapped around it! I tore the paper off, my heart pounding. Was the pearl okay?

It was its regular-size now, still perfect. And the tiny turtle still held the sphere of the pearl between its four webbed feet. I wound the necklace carefully around my wrist and smoothed the paper on my knee.

It was filled with green writing! Turtle writing? Another spell? A clue to the magic?

I read the writing and practically forgot to breathe.

ALL MAGIC IS LINKED
BY HEART AND MIND.
WHAT'S WHITE IS BLACK;
BLACK'S WHITE IN KIND.
ONE IS ALL
AND ALL ARE ONE.

What the heck! It was the words to the song. The song that the turtle sang. But what did they *mean*? I groaned. How come magic spells couldn't be like TV commercials? You know, straight out. The words made no sense to me. I mean, none. And the melody of the song, the melody I knew I'd never forget, was already fading from my mind. What was I supposed to do now? I figured it'd be better if I could get the turtle to help me.

"Hey," I said aloud. "Sir?"

Nothing.

I held the pearl up to the light again. I swung it around. I read the spell or clue or whatever aloud about sixty zillion times.

No magic. No pearl sea.

Well, I must have spent a whole hour, practically, trying to make the magic of the pearl come back. I breathed on it, polished it with Kleenex, sang to it, and swooshed it through the air like a kite.

Still nothing!

No magnificent swimmy pearl space to swim in. No turtle with a voice like God's must be. Just a fading memory of a song that was the most beautiful I'd ever heard and me sitting on the worn-out carpet in my bedroom at Uncle Bart's with a magic spell that made no sense.

ALL MAGIC IS LINKED
BY HEART AND MIND.
WHAT'S WHITE IS BLACK;
BLACK'S WHITE IN KIND.
ONE IS ALL
AND ALL ARE ONE.

Who was the girl on the horse? What was the jewel I was supposed to guard? And how was I going to get Denny to help me?

# CHAPTER

## five

"NATALIE!"

A shout from the open window. I got off the carpet and went to it. Althea stood below on the grass.

"Are you coming down? There's work to do! Bart needs the manure spread, and after that we'll all want to eat."

Yikes! I had to give up, at least for now. I had to get the tractor and the load of manure out to the back field and dump it. I didn't want anybody to know about the magic. If I didn't get out to the barn and start my day, all the people and animals Althea'd gotten out of my room would come stomping right back in wanting to know how come the manure wagon was still full. I hollered to Althea that I'd be right there, then wasted a bunch of time trying to find a clean pair of jeans. Practically all my stuff was in the wash, so I ended up in a pair of jeans I'd left at Uncle Bart's last summer because they were, like, gross, I mean—bell-bottoms! I found a ratty—but clean—T-shirt and gave my barn boots a swipe with a dust rag. I brushed my teeth and all that, and I was finally ready.

Except I had to find a safe place to keep the magic spell and the pearl necklace. Aaagh! I wasted some more time figuring out where this safe place should be. If I wore the necklace, there was a chance that it might break and get lost. If I didn't wear it, maybe the beast would find it when I wasn't around. And the tissue paper for the magic spell was so thin, I didn't want to carry it in my pocket. It might disappear altogether—you just never knew about magic spells. I ended up tucking the spell inside my pillowcase, way back in the corner. I wound the pearl necklace around my wrist; somehow, I knew I had to keep it close to me.

I raced out of the house to the barn.

It was an absolutely gorgeous day outside. Uncle Bart's place was jammed with pickup trucks, horse trailers, people, and horses. Everybody was running around like maniacs to get the riders practiced and ready for the trials. The whole barn staff—John Ironheels, Uncle Bart, Betsy the assistant teacher, and Althea, who helped out part-time when she wasn't teaching us about molecules—would be so busy they might not even have time for lunch. Which was my job—lunch, I mean—when the farm was really busy. I was supposed to make a pile of tuna-fish sandwiches and have them ready for whenever the guys had a chance to eat. After the manure was dumped, of course.

The Kubota tractor was parked where it usually was after the stalls have been mucked out and the wagon filled with the manure. The Kubota was way cool to drive, and when I wasn't in a flap about wizards and magic, I really liked it. I hopped in the seat, pulled out the little knob that ignites the spark plugs, pushed in the clutch, and wiggled the stick that puts the tractor in first gear. Then I stepped on the gas. Driving a manure tractor is not fast; as a matter of fact, a person walking in the regular sort of way is a lot faster. I wasn't allowed to put the Kubota in second gear, since that would let it go as fast as a person jogging. You have to drive slow on account of the weight of the manure wagon. When you dump manure, you drive very slowly out to the field, turn the steering wheel to the right when you get next to the old oak, push in the clutch, and wiggle the shift stick into neutral. Then you push the lever to dump the wagon. The wagon rises up slow in back of you, with a grinding groaning noise, and all the manure slides out in a nice pile. Then you push the wagon back down, put the Kubota into first gear, and drive slowly back to where it was parked in the first place. I did all this, then drove the tractor and wagon back where they belonged. That was one chore accomplished. I had to find Uncle Bart and see about lunch.

Making a living on a horse farm is not as easy as dumping manure. There's a lot more to it. Uncle Bart was Mom's little brother—except he was a whole lot more fun to get along with than *my* little brother—and he worked harder than Mom, Dad, and Aunt

Matty put together. His horse farm was called Still-meadow and it was beautiful. He had three large barns in a U-shape, with a cobblestone yard in the middle. One side of the U was a room for the horse saddles, bridles, and stuff like that. That side had the feed store and the hayloft. Uncle Bart's office was a little room at the very end of this part, under the hayloft. A sign in gold letters on green boards was nailed up over the office door. It said STILLMEADOW FARMS *Specialists in Three-Day Eventing*. The side of the U facing Uncle Bart's office and the feed and hay was the stable. There was room for twenty horses here, including my own favorite mare, Mindy Blue, and Denny's mischievous little pony, Susie.

The bottom of the U was the indoor arena. This is where everyone was this morning. I could see a bunch of people—mostly mothers and like that—standing crowded around the huge opening to the arena. And I could hear the music. Music is very important to riders, especially dressage riders. The rhythm of the music is supposed to match the way the horse moves. I excused myself and got through the crowd of people to where I could see Uncle Bart. I had to find out how many people to make sand-wiches for, which was my next chore for the day. He was standing with two men next to the bleachers. I called out to him, but he didn't hear me because of the music.

The noise in the arena was some of kind march—dah-*dah,* dah-dah-dah-*dah*—and this incredible horse and rider were trotting around the ring to it.

I was bound and determined to talk to Uncle Bart

and tell him I was getting on with my chores, but the sight of that horse and rider stopped me dead in my tracks. The horse was the most beautiful animal I'd ever seen. He was a big white stallion with a silky tail that brushed the ground. He had what Uncle Bart says is a noble head and a kind eye.

A noble head on a horse makes you think of a king or a queen. This horse had small perfect ears, a broad forehead, and a slim nose that flared out into a square jaw and perfectly shaped pink nostrils. You only get this kind of noble head with horses who come from a long line of great winners.

A kind eye is large and colored a clear dark brown. It's the expression that makes it kind, mostly. And kind doesn't mean, like, helpful, when it comes to horses. It means an intelligent, affectionate look. My horse Mindy Blue has an intelligent affectionate look, but I had to say she didn't even come close to the majestic look of this horse. He was awesome.

The girl who was riding him was just as awesome. She was older than I—maybe as much as sixteen. She was an African-American person like my friend Madeline back in Manhattan, except darker. The girl on the horse was this gorgeous black-brown color, like my grandmother's mahogany bureau. She rode so that you couldn't tell which was horse and which was her. It was like they had been born together.

"Wow!" I said. I was so maxed out it didn't seem all that important to do lunch right this second. "Who *is* that?"

One of the mother types in the crowd turned and

looked at me. I guess I had been kind of loud, so I muttered, "Sorry" and kind of backed up.

"That's okay, honey," said this woman, "so are we."

"What d'ya mean, you're sorry?" Denny bulldozed his way through the crowd like one of his Tonka toys.

"Hi, Denny," I said. Then, automatically: "Shut up, Denny."

"What d'ya mean, you're sorry?" Denny demanded. "That's Amanda on her stallion. She's the best rider in the whole place."

The woman sort of curled her lip and turned aside. Denny was even grubbier than ever, but it still made me mad that she sneered at him. He is only six years old, but he deserves respect. He tugged at this snotty woman's denim skirt. "Why should you be sorry about Amanda and her horse?"

The girl and her horse were so beautiful it didn't make much sense to me, either, but somebody else in the crowd kind of snickered. I knew that snicker. It was a Loomis snicker. It had to be either that brat Jeff or that even worse brat, his sister Brett. They were the last kids I wanted to run into. I kind of looked around for a way for Denny and me to escape, but it was too late.

"Yo, Natalie," said Jeff, which was his way of talking cool. He sort of strutted over to where I was standing. "What's happening?"

I figured this didn't even need an answer. I mean, up until yesterday, Brett and Jeff had swanked around like they were gods of the earth because Mr. Loomis held the mortgage on Uncle Bart's farm. Aunt Matty had fixed that pretty quick. She'd paid off Mr. Loomis. I'd hoped Denny and I had seen the last of the Loomis brats, but it was not to be.

"I didn't think you'd be here, Jeff," I said, very standoffish, so he wouldn't get any ideas. The worst thing about Jeff Loomis was that he thought he was *so* cool and *so* cute that any girl within twenty feet of him was just about ready to roll over and die if he flicked his eyelashes. Which actually were pretty cute. That was the problem. Jeff was very cute as long as he didn't open his mouth. A person with any sense forgot all about his great hair and green eyes as soon as he said anything.

"You're kidding, right?" He got this smug superior smarky look on his face. "I'm here because I'm going to ride in the trials on Thursday. I have to practice."

Jeff on the Olympic team? Yeah, right. And I was an FBI agent for *The X-Files*.

"I didn't know you'd qualified." Then I figured since he was obviously still a paying student of Uncle Bart's, I'd better be nice, so I dragged it out of myself. "Congratulations."

"Well, I haven't qualified yet," he said, tossing back his hair like he was Christian Slater and maybe I should faint at his feet. "But my father is having a word with one of the judges. They belong to the same club."

Hah! I didn't know there was a Dork Club right here in Cayuga, New York. But as much as I wanted to, I didn't say it aloud.

The tempo of the music in the arena changed, which meant that the fabulous stallion and his rider were going to do something different. Denny shoved his way in front of me and then leaned back against my legs to watch. The girl on the white horse didn't even seem to breathe, much less move her legs or hands. But the big stallion broke into a collected canter, the three-beat easy gallop that's the most fun of all to ride. In the canter, the horse begins the gait with one foreleg extended before the others. This is called the lead. The lead leg should always be on the inside, so if the right side of the horse is along the wall, the left foreleg leads. In a countercanter, which is hard to get the horse to do, the outside leg leads. This girl had the stallion going so that he changed his leads with each stride. It made an elegant, graceful sight.

The stallion and the girl swept the arena in a perfect circle, wide and easy. The horse led with his left, switched to his right, led with his left, switched to his right in time to the music in the air. The two of them were so beautiful my throat closed up.

"I'll probably be riding that horse, too," said Jeff, watching me out of the corner of his eye. "That is, if that nigger will sell it."

The woman next to me, the one who had called me "honey" and said she was sorry, too, gave Jeff a sort of smirk.

Me, I wanted to fall down a hole and, like, disappear. I couldn't believe he'd said that word. Worse than that word was I couldn't believe this awful woman next to me was looking like she agreed with with this jerk. I mean, where were these two bozos *from*? Mars? I got hot, so I knew I was blushing.

"What's a nigger?" asked Denny.

"A black that's pushing in where she's not wanted," said the woman. "Like that one." She nodded toward the beautiful girl.

"It's an awful word," I said, "that's worse than the F-word or the S-word and you'd better not ever, ever use it, Dennis Carmichael Ross." I couldn't look at this terrible woman. She was an adult. You're supposed to respect adults, unless they're the weird kind that they warn you about in those Don't Trust Strangers programs. Plus, she might be a paying customer and Uncle Bart really needed paying customers to keep his farm successful.

What the heck was I supposed to do? My throat was all tight again, but it wasn't because I'd seen something beautiful. I knew what I could do, though. I gave the horrible Jeff Loomis a kick in the rear end. I aimed too low. He had his riding boots on and my tennis shoe slipped right off of the shiny leather. Then I grabbed Denny and ran off.

I bet I looked like a total fool.

I don't know how I got to Mindy Blue's stall, exactly, because my head was buzzy with total abject humiliation and I couldn't even see straight. I didn't even realize Denny was tagging alongside of me until Mindy Blue snorted, which is her way of saying hello, and I kind of came to. Abject humiliation is the worst. Dad says "abject" means utterly hopeless, miserable, humiliating, and wretched. And that's what I was full of: humiliating humiliation.

"Your face is all red," said Denny in kind of an interested way. I mean, trust a little brother to, like, *care* that you are in an abject state.

"Shut up, Denny," I said.

"It's cool that you kicked Jeff Loomis in the butt. But how come you did it?"

"I didn't kick Jeff Loomis in the butt. I tried to kick him in the butt, but I couldn't even do that right. Anyway, you know enough not to use the word 'butt.' "

"I do?" said Denny. This was not in any rude way, but like he really wanted to know.

"Yes, you do. And I really don't feel like talking to you now, so will you go away? Mindy Blue needs to be brushed."

"She got brushed this morning," said Denny. "Althea did it. And how come sometimes you want me around and sometimes you don't? How come words like 'butt' and 'nig'—"

I clapped my hand over his mouth with one hand. Denny didn't bite, like he usually does. His blue eyes just bugged out. I took my hand away, since I didn't want to suffocate him to death. At least, not very much.

"There are words that hurt people," I said firmly. "And the N-word is one of those. People only use it when then want to disrespect somebody."

This obviously did not mean a whole lot to my little brother. But I had a name for him that he hated more than poison. "How would you like it if I called you 'little boy' all the time?"

Denny scowled and put his dukes up. "I'd punch your lights out."

I grabbed his chubby little wrist. "You'd better not

try," I warned. "Well, the N-word makes people feel like you feel when I call you little boy, only a thousand times worse. It makes people feel abject." I was going to tell him that it was mean to make people feel abject for no reason, but I didn't. "Mean" is not a word that six-year-olds understand very well.

"If it's just a gross thing, how come you didn't do anything? Spiderman would have punched that lady's lights out," Denny said in an accusing way.

Now, all this did was make me feel that *I* should have punched that lady's lights out, and Jeff's, too, which was ridiculous. Jeff was so much bigger than I was he could use me as a floor mop. And try punching an adult and see where *that* gets you. Jail, that's where. Which would be just great. Abject humiliation piled on abject humiliation. I hollered at Denny to beat it. I grabbed a currycomb from the tack box outside Mindy Blue's stall, slid open her door, and slammed in there to brush her.

This was a *very* dumb thing to do. No matter how much you love it and trust it, a horse is still a horse. It is not a person in a horse suit. When a horse is scared or startled, it tries to run away. This comes from the fact that a horse doesn't have fangs, or claws to protect itself from animals that want to kill it and eat it, such as panthers and like that. A horse just slams off and runs when it's scared.

When I ran into that stall waving the brush and hollering at Denny, it scared Mindy Blue.

Her eyes rolled white. She reared to get away. Her hoof came down at me, like somebody'd thrown a huge dinner plate crashing on my head. I shouted, *"No!"* The last thing I remember is an explosion of bright green light. Then the magic swallowed me up.

And there was a blank spot.

# SIX

I WOKE UP IN A STALL FULL OF FURNITURE. AT LEAST it seemed like a stall full of furniture. I blinked. Shook my head to get the fuzzy feeling out. Looked around.

A big old sofa like my grandmother's sat in one corner. The stall wall above this sofa had a whacking big hole in it, so that you could see right into the stall next to Mindy Blue's. The horse in there, a Morgan gelding name Jake, poked his head through the hole. He looked very surprised.

There was more stuff in this stall than sofas. A pot of library paste lay tipped over near a little pile of manure. A bunch of old-timey-looking boots were in a tumble next to some dog chews. A chestnut afghan woven of some hairy stuff was tossed on the sofa arm. There was all kinds of junk in that horse stall. What there wasn't in this stall was a horse.

Mindy Blue was gone.

I got to my feet. Denny grinned at me like a fool from the open stall door. His eyes were green with the magic. My wrist felt funny, as though it had been electrified. I checked it out. The pearl necklace was glowing with a bright green light. I looked back at the afghan. I knew that chestnut color. It was exactly the color of Mindy's mane.

That sofa was horsehair. Those boots were horsehide. And the dog chews—ugh! My brother had turned my horse into a lot of *stuff*!

I, like, totally lost it. I mean, the magic was back, but, jeez! What had it done to my horse? And how come Denny used it without my permission? *"Denny!"* I shrieked. "Dennis Carmichael *Ross*! You bring Mindy Blue back right *now*!" I was so scared for my horse, I grabbed him by the neck and shook him. The pearl necklace clinked against his teeth. He was giggling like a fool. "It's not *funny*!" I yelled.

"Okay, okay, okay, *okay*! Just lemme go, all right?"

I dropped him. Took a deep breath. "Okay. All right. I'm fine now." I looked around the stall again. I never knew they made so many things out of horses. I mean, I know that leather comes from cows and horses and what-all, but *glue*? "Denny, what did you *do*?"

"She was gonna whack you right on the head," he grumbled, like I should maybe have been kissing his feet for disassembling my horse instead of being totally bummed. "She didn't mean it, but her foot—"

"Hoof," I corrected automatically. I noticed that the green in his eyes was fading. The blue was coming back. The magic was going away.

"Okay, *hoof* was coming right down on you. You scared her and there wasn't anywhere for her to go, so I sort of . . . sort of . . ."

"Sort of what?"

He blinked and shook his head a couple of times. His eyes were totally blue now—only a whisper of the magic green in the center. "I can't remember egg-zactly. . . . I pushed the molecules apart."

"Well, you push those molecules together again," I ordered. "Right this minute."

He sighed like it was this big huge deal. Then he just sort of stood there.

"Well?" I demanded.

"I'm not sure egg-zactly how to do it."

"Not sure! How did you do it before?"

He didn't say anything. He didn't even *do* anything. He just stood there perfectly still. This was scary. Almost as scary as having my horse turned into furniture and library paste. Denny's always saying or doing something. He doesn't stand still for two seconds, except when he's asleep, and even then he twitches and thrashes.

"Denny," I said. "Come on and hurry up. We're lucky somebody hasn't found us in this stall with all this stuff already. I mean, what with this being such a busy day in the barn, somebody's going to come down that aisle looking for us pretty soon. You can just bet your life on that."

"Oh. I forgot. Uncle Bart says it's time for lunch. So you're supposed to make sandwiches."

"I'll make you a whole mountain of tuna fish as soon as you magic Mindy Blue back!"

"You're crazy," he said flatly. "I don't want tuna fish, I'm sick of tuna fish. I had tuna fish for breakfast."

I ignored the whole problem of why Denny would eat tuna fish for breakfast. There was this great big huge problem staring me right in the face.

Denny could do magic without me. And he didn't remember how to do it after he did it. The night before, he had magicked the griffin back into people and animal parts. He didn't remember about it this morning. And he didn't remember now, like *seconds* after he'd zapped Mindy Blue. As a matter of fact, the only person who remembered about the magic was me.

What was going on here? I'd just spent all this time in my room trying to call the turtle back and do magic myself. Denny hadn't even thought twice about it; he'd just magicked. I couldn't do the magic, but I knew about it. Denny didn't know about it, but he could do it. The turtle had said, "Together," clear as clear. I knew the truth now:

I couldn't do the magic alone. I wanted to sit right down on the horsehair sofa and cry. I was only part of the magic, not the whole of the magic.

I didn't sit down and cry, of course. There was too much to do—mainly, get Mindy Blue back together again. So I had to get a grip. It looked to me like I was the magic's baby-sitter. I was in charge, to see it did things right.

The pearl necklace was warm on my wrist—like an electric blanket turned up high. Was *that* where the magic was? In the pearl itself? If I took the necklace off, would I forget, like Denny, as soon as it was all over?

I remembered the spell that had come from the pearl:

ALL MAGIC IS LINKED
BY HEART AND MIND.

"Together," the Turtle said. If all magic was linked, maybe that meant there had to be at least two things hooked up together to make the magic work. Maybe even three. Like Denny, the pearl necklace, and me.

"C'mere for a second, Denny."

"I'm hungry. And I don't want tuna-fish sandwiches for lunch. I had tuna fish for break—"

In the depths of the barn, the big door to the outside open slid open. I heard booted footsteps on the concrete aisle. Someone was coming.

"I'll make you peanut butter. Or jelly and pickles. I'll make you anything you want! Just fix this!"

Denny's lower lip jutted out. His face turned so pink the freckles disappeared. In, like, two seconds, I was going to have a major temper tantrum on my hands.

"Hello?" came a voice a couple of stalls away. "Hello? Is anyone here?" The footsteps stopped, hesitated, then turned away in the other direction. I didn't recognize who it was; it sounded like a girl. Whoever it was would find us soon. I had to act quick. If the pearl necklace was the key, maybe Denny had to be touching it, too.

"Quick, Denny. Just slip this over your wrist."

"A bracelet?" Denny hollered, like I'd just asked him to run stark naked through the arena. "I'm not wearing a bracelet!"

*"Ssshh!"*

"If Natalie Ross is here," came the voice, "I've been sent to get her." The footsteps were coming back our way.

I grabbed Denny, pulled him inside the stall, and slid the door shut. We crouched down. Whoever it was walked past the stall. I waited until the sound of footsteps on concrete faded away. Then I unwound the necklace partway from my wrist and slipped the free end of the gold chain around Denny's thumb.

"Do you remember now?" I whispered.

At first, nothing happened. He just glared at me. Then sea green edged his eyes, like a wave creeping onto a beach.

"Mindy Blue?" I said. "Remember Mindy Blue." I thought about my mare. How she knew who I was each time I came back to Uncle Bart's. How much she liked apples. How she liked to run through the wheat fields out back. How awful it would be never to see her again.

"Mindy Blue," Denny said, thoughtful like.

"Mindy Blue," I said.

*Mindy Blue,* came a great calm voice, a voice like a wave of green. *Mindy Blue.*

The turtle was back! The pearl necklace grew and grew, as it had before, that morning. The pearl necklace took me into the the magic with Denny!

We both floated in the shell-pink sea that was the

pearl. The oceany expanse grew and grew until the magic wrapped all around the stall and all the horse stuff in it.

*"Now, Denny!"* I shouted. "Push!"

Denny's eyes flashed green as green. He raised both hands. The pearl necklace fell away from him and wrapped itself around my wrist.

Denny transformed the stall! The sofa, the shoes, each thing inside it became silvery little tornadoes of molecules. The tornadoes whirled and whirled. And Denny pushed the tornadoes together. He pushed again, until they merged into a swirling cyclone in the middle of the stall. Just beyond the cyclone, beyond the pearl sea, through the millions and millions of molecules Denny pushed together, the Morgan gelding Jake watched us through the hole in the stall that had appeared when Denny'd disassembled my horse. Jake pricked his ears. His brown eyes widened.

The horsehair sofa whirled apart. The legs of the sofa re-formed into boards, and the hole Jake was looking through began to fill up again. The horsehide boots spun apart. The afghan disintegrated. The glue sort of oozed into hooves. The specks from all this stuff began to form a shape with four legs and tail, two ears and mane.

*"Hello!"* Jake said as the specks whirled together. *"You're back."*

The last of the stall boards reappeared, flew through the air, and began to wall him up again. "Mindy Blue . . ." I heard Jake say. The hole closed.

The pearl sea was gone. Jake's "Blue" trailed off into a whinny.

My horse stood right where that stupid sofa had been.

# CHAPTER

## SEVEN

FOR A LONG LONG SECOND THERE WAS NO SOUND, NO movement at all.

Then Mindy Blue whickered. I've never been so glad to hear any sound as that one in my whole entire life. She stood there in the stall, warm and golden brown, with the white blaze on her forehead. I stepped forward. Greeny light clung like dandelion seeds to her mane. I touched them. Her mane was silky warm beneath my hand. The green light flared briefly and then began to float away.

I took a deep breath. All of Mindy's parts seemed to be in place: her hooves were on the right way; the little white sock on her left hind leg was back; even the little scar on her hock from an old wire cut was there. She looked great. A little puzzled, but great. I checked her over again, just to be sure. She was just fine. No cuts, no bruises, and she nudged her head into my chest like she always does when we spend time in her stall together.

I turned to my brother, the wizard. There was no question about it now, that was for sure. Denny was a wizard. A possibly dangerous one. And I was in charge. Suddenly I didn't want to be in charge at all. This was just too scary. I backed up a bit, just in case he was dangerous right now. He looked just like he always does. Grubby. Sweaty. His red hair sticking up all over. And the sign of the magic—the color of his eyes—had disappeared. I reached out to touch him—a little hesitantly. It's not every day you get proof positive that you and your six-year-old bratty brother can shove the very molecules of the world around—and that you have to control it with a pearl necklace that could, like, break, or get lost anytime.

"I'm hungry," Denny complained. "I'm starved. I'm so starved that I'm going to croak right here on the floor. I want to eat."

"Just hush up a second," I said. "I want to make sure Mindy's okay."

There was a tap on the stall door. That girl was back. She called, "Hello? Anyone in there?"

"Just a minute!" I answered. I quickly looked around. Everything that Denny had separated Mindy into was gone. I tucked the pearl necklace into my jeans pocket and slid open the door,

It was the beautiful rider from the arena.

"Hi," she said. "I'm Amanda Sadik. That's not like it sounds, by the way. It's spelled S-A-A-D-I-Q. Saadiq. Are you Natalie?"

There's a certain look top riders have. Even when they're walking on their own two feet, they look like they're riding an invisible horse. I think it's because they're tall, mostly, and they have long legs, with these great muscles. These riding muscles give them a special sort of walk, like they're gliding slightly from side to side as they go. They stand really straight, just like they sit on a horse; shoulders back, spine upright. Uncle Bart told me once that top riders act like a rope is tied right beneath their ribs and pulled straight up to their chins. I stuck my own shoulders back, pretended I had a rope tied right under my belt buckle, and stood up straight. "Hi," I said.

She laughed a little, not much, and in a nice way, really. I could feel my face getting hot, and I knew it was probably pink, but I just went and blurted out, "I saw you in the arena today. On that stallion. It was awesome!"

She chuckled out loud. It was a rich sound. Not like her talking voice, which was light and pretty. She said, "It's the horse more than me, girl." Then sort of a calm look came over her, like she'd put on a different face than the one she just showed me. "His name is Sooley mon." Or something like that.

"Sooley mon," said Denny. "That's a weird name."

I poked him to shut up. Denny's idea of polite is that he doesn't pick his nose and eat it in front of adults.

"It's Suleiman," she said, spelling it out. "The horse is named after a great Ottoman chief, Suleiman the Magnificent. A wise man, and a wise horse."

Behind me, Mindy Blue blew out with a sound like, "Whhhrrrr."

"And who's this?" asked Amanda. She moved

lightly forward. She reached out to Mindy Blue, palm up. Mindy stuck her nose into her hand and blew out again.

"She likes you," Denny said, suddenly very bossy. "She only does that when she likes somebody. Natalie, I'm *hungr*—"

I poked him again. "Amanda knows all about horses, Denny. So don't you go thinking you can tell her a thing. And we'll get lunch in just a minute, okay?" I turned back to Amanda. I'd never really gotten a chance to talk to a great rider before, and I wasn't about to blow it just to make my little brother a peanut-butter sandwich.

"This your horse?" Amanda asked She ran her hand under Mindy's muzzle, then up around her ears. She rubbed the mare between the eyes. Mindy closed her eyes and drooped her lower lip, which is what she does when she's happy.

"Yes. I mean, not really. She's Uncle Bart's. But she's mine to ride when we stay here."

"Bart told me you spend the summers at Stillmeadow. You like to ride?"

"I love it." Then like a dumb fool, I went ahead and blurted, "I'd like to learn to ride like you."

"Would you?"

"Would I!" All my dreams came rushing back. The dreams that sent me to sleep the night before with a grin on my face. Natalie the Great! Rider of the Year! The only thirteen-year-old gold medalist in equestrian history!

Amanda smiled, "We'll have to ride out together sometime."

"That'd be great," I said. "When? You want to go this afternoon? Or right now, maybe? I could get Mindy tacked up pretty fast."

She nodded, "Well, we could at that. But I'll tell you. I worked Suleiman pretty hard this morning, and I just turned him out into the paddock for a nice roll in the sand and a little relaxation. And your uncle's going to want you to bring him his lunch pretty soon, isn't he?"

"*Yes!*" shouted Denny.

I was embarrassed. Of course I had things to do. I wasn't going to be much of a wizard's boss if I couldn't get my regular stuff done.

"You go on, then." She smiled, not really at me, if you know what I mean, but in my general direction. "We'll meet again, I know."

She strolled away down the aisle. I watched her go. She looked so cool, it was unbelievable. Her black hair was in a tight, smooth bun in the back. She had tiny gold earrings in her ears. Her skin was a little darker than Mindy's coat, with just a little more gold. I wished I could ride like she could. I wished I *looked* like she did, as though nothing on this earth could drive her bonkers. As though she never got a zit, or cried for no reason, or had to pretend she didn't care when she did incredibly dumb things.

"Maybe you could be like that, Natalie Ross," I whispered to myself. "Maybe you and Denny and the magic . . ."

My brain was buzzing. I closed my eyes. I could see it now. Mindy and me, trotting around the Olympic arena. The Olympic jumps would be huge—five feet six inches high, at the very least. I would lean forward and whisper in Mindy's ear, "Jump now, girl, jump now!" And Mindy would soar like a bird, the magic giving her wings. We would float through those jumps like—well, like magic. And at the end, after we'd jumped five feet, six feet, maybe more, I would get off in the winner's circle and walk like Amanda walked, tall straight and proud, to get the blue ribbon.

I opened my eyes. Mindy was nosing at her hay bag for hay. Denny was trying to unscrew her water bucket from the stall wall, just for something to do, the little brat. I pulled him away from the bucket, ignoring his wriggling.

I was going to *make* him fix up me and my horse. Right now.

I checked out Mindy Blue one more time to make sure that she was okay. Everything in the stall was the way it was supposed to be. The afghan had turned back into her mane, the sofa had turned back into her shiny chestnut coat, and the library paste back into her hooves. There weren't any dog chews around, which was fine by me because I wasn't sure I wanted to know what part of Mindy Blue they had been. The oak boards behind her had gotten caught up in the magic—to make the frame of the sofa, I guess, and they were all in place.

I ran the whole series of events through my mind again, just to make sure that Denny'd been okay, that Mindy hadn't been hurt, and that Jake . . .

Jake! I gasped. Jake had talked! Jake looked

through the hole in the wall and said, "Welcome back" to Mindy Blue.

Denny's magic makes horses talk!

I was so excited I almost swallowed my spit. I decided then and there that the first thing this magic was going to do was make Mindy Blue talk to me. Then Denny would change us. And then . . . and then . . . I stood on my toes and whispered in her ear, "We'll find out, girl. We'll find out how to win the Olympics."

Mindy rolled her eye at me.

"Okay, Denny. Here's what I want you to do."

"You want me to eat lunch."

"Not now."

"Yes, now!"

"We're going to turn Mindy Blue into the kind of horse Amanda's got. Only a mare, of course. We're going to turn her into a champion."

"No. I don't want to."

If I had a quarter for every time I've heard "I don't want to" from Denny, I could buy three Olympic horses. I grabbed Denny by the arm and pulled him toward Mindy. He was going to help me whether he wanted to or not. I must have grabbed him too hard because he yelled "ow!" like he really meant it and wasn't just busting my chops. I think he started to cry, but I was too excited to really pay attention.

Then—for a second, just a second—something in the air of the barn moved, like a giant shadow, or the wing of a huge, ugly bird. And it was cold. I grabbed the pearl necklace, and it was cold, too. Mindy jerked her head up and backed into the far corner of the

stall, her eyes rolling white. Denny stopped crying
and turned so white his freckles stuck out.

I dropped the necklace like it bit me. The beast.
The beast was back.

# eight

I HAD A SUDDEN, HORRIBLE, ELECTRIC SORT OF FEEL-ing all over me. Just like when I grabbed the electric horse fence the first time I'd visited Uncle Bart.

*Did I bring the beast? Did it show up when I wanted something I didn't really deserve?*

"No," I said. "That's ridiculous. I just want . . ."

It was my imagination, wasn't it? That cold, cold hissing.

"Hey!" said Denny in this little voice. "Do you hear that?" He took one step, then another. Away from me. Toward that . . . Thing.

"Denny," I said. "Stop."

Denny cocked his head, as if he were listening. "Okay," he said.

"Okay, what?" I lifted him in my arms and held him. His face was perfectly white. His eyes were dead. Dead and cold. "Denny? *Denny!*"

He didn't answer. He looked over my shoulder. He

reached out one hand. I felt it. On the back of my neck. A hand like a bone. Like ice. I whirled, Denny in my arms. I couldn't see a darn thing. Nothing. Just that feeling of darkness. "Beat it, you!" I said, as fierce as I could. My heart was shaking my whole body. I couldn't get my breath, I was so scared. "Beat it. *Beat it!*"

Mindy whinnied. Jake whinnied. The whole barn echoed and reechoed with the sounds of the horses. From way outside, I heard Suleiman's stallion cry.

Dirty light fluttered, like wings beating to escape. *"You stay away from my brother!"*

The shadow withdrew. The barn fell silent. Denny started to breathe again in my arms. He blinked. The color in his face was back. I set him down before I dropped him. My arms and legs were shaking so much I thought I was going to fall over.

"Are you all right, Denny?"

"Sure? Can you fix lunch now?"

"Are you *sure* sure? You didn't—um—see anything? Or hear anything?"

"I heard my stomach. It says, 'Feed me now!' "

"Right. Two seconds. Are *you* okay, girl?" I said to Mindy. My voice was kind of sticking in my throat, so I cleared it and said louder, "Okay, girl?"

Mindy found a bit of hay and began to munch. With the Thing gone, my mind began to work again. I'd actually grabbed Denny so hard it hurt him. All because I wanted to be a star and he wanted lunch. I could maybe see that being the wizard's boss was going to be hard.

I was too bummed to look at Denny at first, but

then I knelt down in front of him and wiped his face with a Kleenex from my pocket. "Sorry," I said. "I didn't mean . . . well . . . sorry." Denny was like, oblivious. I began to be glad he forgot about the magic once he used it. I'd hoped he'd forgotten everything: including how rotten I was. I felt just awful about grabbing him like that. Something had definitely gotten into me—and it wasn't good.

Not to mention that horrible beast I'd just felt. I did not want to think about this beast. No way. I, like, shoved that beast to the back of my brain and tried to think good thoughts.

Nothing much came to me. Just all the applause and the silver trophy and the thrill of being a winner. Dad says that being logical is the way to make good decisions. So I tried to be logical. "How could it hurt, girl?" I asked Mindy. "If Denny wanted to help me be a winner, that wouldn't be a bad use of the magic, would it? We could still be winners in a nice way, couldn't we? And you, you'd want to be a star, too, wouldn't you?"

She snorted. I just bet she agreed with me. I just bet you could use that magic in a good way, if you went about it right.

I thought logically about using Denny's magic to change Mindy Blue. What if something happened? There was more to this magic stuff than was totally obvious. What if the molecules got confused about whether they were shoe or horse bits? Would I have a horse with leather Nikes instead of hooves? No, that wouldn't happen. As far as I could tell, Denny couldn't change horse molecules into dog molecules or like that—but he could rearrange the shape of things, using the same stuff. So he could, like—make a five-legged Mindy, who'd be a lot shorter, of course, since Denny didn't seem to be able to add or subtract the amount of bone molecules. If Denny didn't know exactly how to make a winner horse, this could be a serious problem. Logically, I would have to make a list.

Denny was making these incredibly obnoxious gagging sounds like he was going to fall over dead any minute from hunger. So the next thing on my list wasn't magic, it was lunch. I'd skipped breakfast, what with messing around with the pearl necklace and all, and I was getting pretty hungry myself. Maybe food would keep my brain from feeling like warm Jell-O and help me be logical instead of emotional.

I kept an eye on Denny as we walked out of the barn and back to the house. He seemed okay. I took a couple of deep breaths: that had been a narrow escape. I was going to have to be very careful from now on. This magic was powerful stuff.

The crowd around the arena door was even thicker than before. I caught sight of Brett Loomis's blond hair sticking up in the middle of a bunch of little kids. She was dressed totally perfectly as usual. She was wearing the new kind of stretchy white riding breeches, polished black hunting boots, and a crisp white rat-catcher blouse. It was too hot for anyone to be wearing a show coat, but she had hers on anyhow, and I couldn't see a drop of perspiration on her anywhere.

She hadn't seen me yet, and I sure didn't want her to. I grabbed Denny's hand to make him go faster, which was my first mistake. He hollered, "Cut it out," which meant he was perfectly normal again, thank goodness, except that when Denny shrieks, it's like six fire engines at once. Brett turned around when she heard Denny shriek, just like everybody else did. She waved at me and plastered on this big fake smile. I decided to totally ignore Brett Loomis, which was my second mistake. There are some kind of people, if you ignore them, they, like, want to get into your face even more.

"Natalie!" she hollered. Well, cooed out, really. She sounded just like one of those big fat pigeons that hang out at Central Park. Trust Brett Loomis to be too perfect to do such a thing as holler out loud. "Oooohhh, Nataleee!"

A few of the adults standing near her gave her big approving smiles. I hate it when an adult gives some kid like Brett Loomis big approving smiles. They never see the things she really does, like practically walking right over a little kid who was standing in her way, which she did to Denny.

"Hi, Brett," I said when she came up. She was wearing perfume, for Pete's sake. At a horse barn!

"I missed seeing you today, Natalie."

I looked at her sideways. Brett Loomis had never, ever wanted to be seen with me before. She was way too cool. I wondered what she wanted.

She fell in step beside me, pushing Denny aside in a way she thought I couldn't see. Denny stopped short. Looked mad. Then got a thoughtful expression on his face. I didn't do anything about this expression. I'd seen it on Denny before. He was cooking something up. Which was okay by me. I hoped that whatever it was, it'd be a dilly.

"Going up to the house?" Brett asked, just as sweet as pie.

"I have to make lunch for the guys," I said. "Excuse me."

"Maybe I can help?"

This stopped me in my tracks. "Help?" I echoed.

"Well, it must be quite a lot of work, making lunch for—how many people?"

"Uncle Bart, Aunt Matty . . ." I counted under my breath. Amanda, John Ironheels, Denny, and me. Althea and Betsy the trainer. "Eight people."

"Nine including me, right? So you could use my help."

"I guess." I looked at her sideways again. So that was what she wanted: to suck up to Uncle Bart and the trainers. "Usually the most help I need is cleaning up the kitchen. Doing the dishes and stuff like that."

That didn't faze her one little bit. "Sure!" she said. What the heck, if I could make Brett Loomis do dishes, that was fine by me. She kept following me, right past the arena, the office with the sign that read STILLMEADOW FARMS, and past the fenced paddocks. Then Brett grabbed my arm all of a sudden. "Look," she said. "Isn't he beautiful?"

I hated to agree with Brett Loomis about anything, but I had to agree with her about this. Suleiman the Magnificent stood by himself in the paddock farthest from the barns. He stood with his neck arched, his eyes wide, gazing into the green distance. The breeze made his silky mane wave like a silver scarf. He turned his head when we stopped, then walked toward the fence.

Even Denny the garbage disposal forgot about lunch for a second. The three of us went to the fence and hung over it.

"Here-boy, here-boy," Brett cooed in this awful voice. She held out her hand, palm up, like you're supposed to do when you meet a horse. Suleiman walked right up to her. He put his muzzle into her hand and snorted. Then he backed up. He pawed the ground with one elegant leg and shook his head, like horses do when they don't like something. I knew what he didn't like was the perfume smell. But Brett must have thought he didn't like her.

Brett looked cross. "Stupid thing," she said. "I'll bet Jeff will teach him a thing or two."

"That's Amanda's horse," Denny said.

Brett just looked smug. I remembered what her ratty brother Jeff had said that morning—that Mr. Loomis was going to buy Suleiman.

"He is not a stupid thing. It's probably your perfume. Horses don't like the smell of perfume. Here, boy." I always carry carrots in my pockets. If you want to catch a horse each and every time you've got to get it out of the pasture, it's smart to carry a treat. So I dug a carrot out of my pocket and reached out to the stallion.

"He's not going to eat that nasty old vegetable." Brett sniffed. "It looks like it's a million years old.

And it smells like manure. As a matter of fact, you both smell like manure."

This is not a big deal, if you ask me. I mean, Denny and I had been messing around with magic in a horse stall, and that's what in them, usually. Manure.

Suleiman the Magnificent liked the way I smelled all right. He walked right up to me and put his nose in my hand. He didn't take the carrot right away, just sniffed gently at my hand and then blew out a little. His breath was warm. The pearl necklace buzzed a little.

Magic? I thought. Magic now? Right here in front of everyone?

I got nervous. Then I got excited. Was Suleiman going to talk to me? Right here? In front of everyone? I would do almost anything to have a horse talk to me. Denny's magic in the barn had let Jake say "hello" and "welcome back" to Mindy Blue.

I stood there, dreams in my head. Denny, the pearl necklace, and me. Could we do it? Could we magic Mindy Blue so that she could talk all the time? Could the magic help me talk to all horses?

I stared at Suleiman. He stared back, his great eyes flashing. "Hey, boy," I said softly. "Hey."

Uncle Bart says that horses will talk to you any old day of the week if you know how to listen. Right now Suleiman talked to me in the way horses talk to all humans. A soft breath out means "hello." A snort means "I don't think I like this." A whinny is a call to another horse. Suleiman said hello to me in the way all horses do, by breathing into my palm.

"Hmmph," said Brett Loomis.

Suleiman's nose was as soft as clouds must be. His kind eye looked into mine. Denny nudged me, suddenly, and grabbed my other hand. The pearl necklace got hotter and hotter. A greenish mist seemed to film over the sun.

I sneaked a look at Brett. She hadn't noticed a thing!

A voice sounded in my head: not the turtle, whose voice was like God's must be. But a strong voice—a voice like mahogany wood.

I gasped. It was Suleiman!

*you will leave the mare, as herself, my daughter.*

I stood there like a fool, looking back.

*do you understand? you must not trifle with the way things are. you must obey the Law, as we all do.*

The Law?

*promise.*

I was in, like, awe. I was doing it. I was talking to this stallion. I mean, it was in my head. Telepathy, like. But I was doing it!

Brett was reaching over the fence, patting his neck. Through the misty green all over, I could see people going about the regular barn business. I was in the middle of the magic, and no one could see!

And Suleiman wanted me to promise not to use the magic to help with this awesome thing? Promise not to become an Olympic rider? And no one would even be able to tell that it was magic that was doing it? No!

Suleiman pawed the earth. *promise!*

"I . . ." I said. I was like choking, I was so bummed out. "I . . . can't! I can't promise!"

*Aahhh.*

There was sadness all around me. From the horse. From the pearl. I started to shake. I felt scared and ashamed. But a promise is a big thing. If I promised, I couldn't go back on it. Not ever.

"How come?" I asked. I mean, I was begging, here. "Why do I have to promise? If I could just know how come . . . I understand about not being mean. I understand about not hurting other people to do it. But if Denny wants to help me—why not?"

Suleiman blew out—a discouraged, angry sound.

*things fall apart; the center cannot hold.*

The giant voice was muffled, like a big scarf was in the way, and I couldn't hear much of the next part, because the voice faded in faded out, like a bad TV transmission. This was okay with me. I was pretty sure I didn't want to hear what was coming next. I didn't understand what was coming now.

*and what rough beast, its hour come round at last, slouches towards Bethlehem to be born?*

Okay. Great. If I didn't promise not to break this law, that beast was going to get me? Or worse yet, Denny?

I felt like crying, right there in the middle of the magic. How could I promise not to use the magic when I didn't understand?

"Promise what?" whined bratty Brett Loomis. I could barely hear her through the swirl of magic. Couldn't she see it? Couldn't she hear it? The pearl necklace was hot in my pocket, like a fiery coal from a furnace. The green mist was all around me. "What are you sorry about?"

The magic dimmed. Ebbed away like water.

Brett waved her hand in front of my face, like there were flies there. "Earth to Natalie," she said, like this was hilarious. "Earth to Nat—"

"Stop it!" I said.

"Well, excuse me!"

I was not in the best mood in the world, I admit it. So I called Brett a pretty good cussword. "You brat."

"Shut up."

"No, *you shut up!*"

We glared at each other. She obviously hadn't heard or seen a thing about the magic.

Brett tossed her perfect blond hair. "What do you think you're doing, anyway? That horse belongs to my brother."

"Not yet, he doesn't." I looked at Suleiman. He stood in the paddock, brighter than the sun.

Denny tugged at my hand. "Let's go," he said. He had a serious look.

Had Denny heard the stallion talk to me in my mind? Had Denny known what I wanted him to do to Mindy Blue—change her, make her more . . .

A mere fading whisper now, the mighty voice in my mind: *you would make her less. she is what she is. and she is good at what she is. do not meddle with her spirit.*

"Let's go before Brett busts you in the chops," Denny said.

I blinked at Brett Loomis, who was tapping her boot on the ground like she was some big deal. I looked down at Denny. The magic was going through him. I could see that. The greenish light lay softly in his eyes. But the magic went through Denny like water through a pipe. No. His magic didn't talk to him. He didn't really understand it.

Would it be a terrible thing to change Mindy Blue into an Olympic horse? Would it be like saying I didn't love her for what she was? Would it be stupid to change myself into a rider like Amanda Saadiq? I'd be beautiful and graceful and the world would know me as the greatest of them all. What would be so terrible about that?

Except that I was maybe a little bit like Brett Loomis, in wanting something I hadn't earned?

I was more bummed than I had ever been in my whole life. What good was this magic? One thing I knew for sure. The whole thing was going to be a whacking pain in the neck. Because all Denny could do was use it. He didn't understand it. He was too little. I couldn't use it, but I was responsible for it. Logical thinking wasn't going to help all that much, either. Because along with the logic was some kind of law about how you couldn't mess with the spirit of things. If you just thought logically without thinking of the other person, or horse, in the case of Mindy Blue, you could get into trouble.

This is what I understood, now: I couldn't let Denny use the magic for selfish reasons to change the way things were supposed to be. If there was any other stuff I wasn't supposed to do with the magic—I'd just have to find out—and keep the beast away while I did it.

## CHAPTER

# nine

THE MAGIC GREEN MIST IN FRONT OF MY EYES cleared. Suleiman the Magnificent moved away. He dropped his nose to the grass in the paddock and began to graze. I was shaking like Jell-O.

"Watch and be warned," was Suleiman's message. "Watch out for the rough beast."

Brett's whiny voice penetrated the mist of misery in my mind. "Natalie! Come on. I see a bunch of people headed up to the house. They're going to be expecting lunch. I told you I'll help you." She dusted her hands against her new breeches. "There's a place for me to wash up, isn't there?"

I didn't answer her right away. I was looking at Denny. He'd found some bubble gum in his pocket or wherever—yesterday's probably, since he likes to keep the same piece of gum for a week or so—and was chewing it in big slurpy globs. Loving your little brother is not something you blabber on about, be-

cause it's, like, so sappy. But I did love Denny. A lot.
I wouldn't let that beast get him for all the Gold Medals in the universe.

Brett poked me on in the side. "I can't make lunch
all dirty like this! I mean, I'm filthy. Can I use your
bathroom, at least?"

I scowled at her. "Yeah. Sure. Yeah."

"Good. I'll get my purse. I'll meet you in the
kitchen."

I looked toward the farmhouse. Brett was right.
There was a whole pile of people headed toward the
house, and they were expecting food! I started off at
a run. Denny zoomed alongside of me, and we almost
got there before everyone else did. Not quite.

"Well, Natalie!" said Uncle Bart. "I haven't had a
chance to see you all morning!" He stepped over and
gave me a hug. I gave him a big one back. Uncle Bart
is the youngest of my uncles, and he is definitely the
best. He has bright blue eyes, a face that's tanned all
the time from being outside with the horses, and a
totally cool attitude. He has that special horseback
rider's walk, round and elegant.

"Lunch'll be ready in a minute," I said. I looked
around, counting how many sandwiches I would
need. There was Althea, of course, who helps out
with Uncle Bart when she's not tutoring us, and
Betsy, the assistant trainer. Then there was John
Ironheels, thank goodness, in his black hat and long
braids. He was Uncle Bart's barn manager. He was
also an Onondaga Indian and a wise man of his tribe.
I'll bet that he would know about how to use this
magic in the right way.

He looked at me and winked. Almost like he'd read my mind!

And there was Amanda, looking beautiful and calm, but not part of the group. She was sitting off by herself, hands in her lap.

So, there'd be eight people for lunch. Nine if you counted the horrible Brett. That was a lot of sandwiches. Uncle Bart must have seen this, like, dismayed look on my face. "You going to need some help in the kitchen, Nat?"

"Here I am!" Brett said in this gooey way. "Here to help, Mr. Loomis!"

She was carrying her purse with her. And she'd tied a gorgeous white sweater over her shoulders, so that she looked just . . . perfect.

I tucked my T-shirt into my jeans, scrubbed my hair back with both hands, and marched into the kitchen.

"What shall I do first?" Brett asked in this very social way, like she was maybe forty-two years old.

"You can get out the bread," I said. "We'll need nine sandwiches, so that's eighteen slices. Two loaves."

"I want two sandwiches," Denny demanded.

"You never eat more than a half a sandwich, Denny."

"I want *two*!" Denny yelled.

"Why don't we make two each," said Brett, which wasn't such a bad idea. I was starved, myself. "Is the bathroom this way? I'll be back in a second. Go on and get started without me."

Well, she wasn't back in anywhere near a second,

of course. She stayed in that bathroom doing goodness knows what all the whole time Denny and I
made all those sandwiches. Taking off all that perfect makeup and slathering it on again, like she does
a dozen times a day.

My little brother and I are pretty good at making
lunch. Denny lays the bread out, I put the stuff on
the bread, and Denny smacks the sandwich together,
cuts it in half, and puts it on a plate. I made a gallon
of lemonade from a mix. Althea had made a whole
bowl of potato salad the night before, and there was
a huge plate of fresh strawberries from the garden.
Denny talked me into opening an extra-large-size
bag of potato chips, so by the time Miss Queen of the
Universe emerged from the bathroom, we had a
pretty good lunch ready.

When we carried all the stuff in, you would have
thought good old Brett had been right alongside of
us, slaving away instead of squirting perfume all
over herself for twenty minutes. "Tuna fish, Mr. Ironheels?" she said, sweet as pie, offering the plate to
John. "Peanut butter, Althea? I'm sorry I didn't have
time to cut the crusts off." Then she passed around
the lemonade like she was pouring champagne or
something, and sat right next to Uncle Bart, chat-
tering away like she was some big social bee. Sucking
up to the trainers, just like I figured.

Denny came and sat down so close to me he was
practically in my lap. He does this when there are
a lot of people around, so I didn't think too much
about it. I didn't even think too much about it
when the necklace began to buzz in my jeans pocket.

I chomped away at a peanut-butter sandwich, thinking hard about all that had happened. So I didn't smell it at first. Uncle Bart was the first to notice it.

"Anybody smell anything?" He wrinkled his nose. "Ugh!" He stopped eating his tuna-fish sandwich, opened it up, and sniffed it. "It's not that, thank goodness. What *is* that smell, Thea?"

It *was* an awful smell. Like dead something. Althea wrinkled her nose, too. "I don't know. Fish fertilizer, maybe?"

Betsy the assistant trainer shrugged and took another sandwich. She was kind of old—maybe thirty—and skinny, but she ate all the time. "Smells more like fish oil," she said.

Uncle Bart gave Brett a kind of funny look. Then he said, "Excuse me," in this very polite way and got up and moved across the porch. Now the closest person to Brett was Althea. Althea stared at her, frowned a little bit, opened her mouth to say something, then ate some potato chips instead.

The breeze came up. By now, this smell was stinking up the place like you wouldn't believe.

It was coming from Brett!

She sniffed. Then sniffed again. Her face turned red. She wriggled around in her chair, flipped her hair back with one hand, and tried to look like nothing was wrong at all.

"Fish barf," said Denny. "That's fish barf I smell. Can you smell it, Natalie? Boy, does it stink." He started making these big exaggerated sniffing sounds, then bounced up from his chair and started sniffing everybody on the porch. He had peanut butter all over his face. He looked perfectly disgusting. "I smell . . ." he said in the voice you use when pretending to be the giant in a fairy story. "Fee-fie-fo-fum! I smell the fishy blood of . . ." He whirled and pointed a finger at Brett, who was now this bright scarlet color. *"You!"* Denny roared. "I smell . . . *fish barf.*"

"What you smell, Denny," said John Ironheels, "is whale ambergris."

Amber-gris? What the heck was amber-gris?

John looked directly at me, just like I'd said it aloud. "It's what happens when you take the molecules of any expensive perfume apart."

"It's an opaque, ash-colored secretion of the sperm-whale intestine," added Althea in her tutor voice.

Yuck!

John turned around and faced Brett. "And it appears to be all over you, Miss Loomis."

"Fish barf," said Denny. "Cool."

I had a sudden, awful thought. "Be warned," the stallion had said. I thought Denny couldn't use the magic without me knowing about it. But he'd sat right next to me, smack against my jeans pocket where I kept the necklace. So we'd been linked. And here he'd gone and taken apart Brett's perfume! I went cold all over at the thought of a six-year-old wizard who thought Spiderman should be president of the United States. He *could* take apart the world! And he didn't even have to ask me about it. And he wouldn't know enough to protect himself from the beast!

# ★★★ CHAPTER ★★★

## ten

"EXCUSE ME." I JUMPED OUT OF MY CHAIR, KNOCKING over the potato chips and spilling the salads. It was a good thing we were all out on the porch.

"Natalie?" asked Uncle Bart. "What's—"

"I just have to go upstairs. For a second. I . . ." I searched for a really good excuse. "I just have to write something down. For our tutoring lesson this afternoon." I raced for the kitchen door, then turned back. "Sorry about the salad. I'll clean it up as soon as I get back."

As I ran upstairs I heard the horrible Brett whine, "That girl is *so* clumsy! Look at what she's spilled! She must have spilled this whale stuff all over *me*— and . . ."

I lost the whine once I reached the stair landing and skidded into my room. I scrambled for pencil and paper. What Suleiman had given me was a spell, or a clue, I didn't know which. But I had to write it down before I forgot the whole thing. I had to find out how to keep Denny from using the magic and calling the beast by mistake. I didn't bother with a chair but sprawled right on the ratty old carpet.

### THINGS FALL APART.

I remembered that all right. I wrote that down. Then there was something about the center.

### THE CENTER DOES NOT HOLD.

Like, the Center for Adult Living my grandfather went to to play cards? Or Lincoln Center, where we saw the mouse ballet at Christmas? Or maybe the center was the middle, like the white part of an Oreo. When the goo wasn't in there, the cookie fell apart.

### WHAT ROUGH BEAST . . .

I couldn't remember the rest of the beast part. I grabbed the pearl necklace for safety, just thinking about the beast. Then I stuck the necklace back in my pocket, fast. Maybe using the pearl necklace would bring the beast.

It was a furry beast, as I recalled, so I wrote *What manners does this furry beast have?*—which wasn't right, but close enough. I got spooked again about the giant shadow in Mindy's stall. Was it a beast with wings?

This was getting too much for me. All of a sudden I wanted to crawl under my bed and stay there. Especially with a beast hanging out ready to jump on me and my dorky little brother any second now.

"Natalie?" Althea tapped on the door and opened it at the same time. This is an aggravating things adults do, because it doesn't give a person enough time to put on a normal face if they have to.

Althea walked in and sat down on the rug next to me. "You okay?"

"Yeah." I folded the paper where I'd written the spell or whatever it was.

"What's this?" Althea tapped gently on the paper. Her fingernails were a little grimy, which is what happens when a person spends a a lot of time around horses.

"Some stuff I wrote."

"Can I see it?"

I thought about this. Not everyone could *see* the magic. I knew that after having talked to Suleiman right out in front of everybody. That Brett hadn't noticed a thing. The magic didn't stick in anybody's brain but mine, either. Even Denny didn't remember what he'd done after he'd done it. So it might be safe to show her Suleiman's message after all.

I unfolded the paper. She took it and read it. She looked, like, very surprised.

"You wrote this?"

I had a very big hunch that now was not the time to fib, even though this might blow the secret of the magic. Actually, there aren't too many times to fib. When Aunt Matty gives you a perfectly horrible pair of tennis shoes that light up when you walk, *that's* the time to lie. You say, "Thank you Aunt Matty, I

love them," and lie through your teeth. But if somebody asks you where did you get this, you have to
say where.

"I heard it somewhere." I must have given Althea
kind of an anxious look, because she patted my hand.
"Only I don't think I heard it right."

"No. You didn't hear it quite right. It's a wonderful
poem. . . ."

"A poem?"

"A great poem. By a man named William Butler
Yeats. I won't give you all of it, because I can't remember much past the first verse." She sat up a little
straighter and blabbered on about birds and pools of
blood and like that, in a very solemn way, the way
people read poems. It was totally gross. The poem I
mean. Also I didn't understand a word of it. She
stopped blabbering and I asked, "What about the
furry monster?"

"The rough beast. 'What rough beast, its hour come
round at last, towards Bethlehem to be born?' "

"That's the one. What kind of beast is it, anyway?
And where's it from?"

I didn't need to know where it was going. It was
okay by me that this beast was slouching toward
somewhere other than Cayuga Lake. I just wanted
to make sure it didn't slouch on over to me. Or
Denny.

Well, Althea started tutoring.

And it wasn't even time for our lesson yet. Hooray.

She said about how a word means different things
than what you think it meant and that "rough" didn't
mean furry or not-smooth but, like, very very crude

and primitive. And rotten, too, because the point of this whole poem was that the monster was all the bad stuff people do coming down on top of their heads like a thunderstorm. I asked her a couple of questions, like does this monster have claws, and wings, and sharp teeth and like that. Althea patted my hand and said it was a metaphor.

"A meta-for," I said, in a very impressed way. I was tired of this conversation and I wanted her to stop tutoring so I could think about the magic some more and maybe get it straightened out.

"Metaphor." She spelled it. "It's a figure of speech that is used to mean something else."

Hooray again. "Why not just say it straight out?"

"Because it's not as cool," Althea said, which shows she has some sense as a tutor. "It's accurate to say that Suleiman jumps very well. It's very cool to say Suleiman's an eagle, soaring over the jumps. It makes you think more of the poetry of the way he moves. Suleiman's not really an eagle. He's a horse. But he's an eagle when he flies under Amanda, that's for sure."

"So this hairy beast—"

"Rough beast."

"Rough beast. Which is all the bad things that come onto people . . ."

"War. Gang fights. Drugs. All kinds of cruelty that people do to each other."

"What would this beast look like? If it's a combination of all that stuff?"

"Umm." Althea thought a little bit. "I suppose I don't know. Just think that'd it be the most horrible thing you could imagine. Which isn't a very good answer. I'm sorry, Natalie."

Sorry? We were all going to be more than sorry if this beast showed up at Uncle Bart's horse farm.

"In a way," said Althea, "you could say this beast is a lack of rules. Kay-os," or something like that. She spelled it out. "C-H-A-O-S. It means total confusion. That's why the poet was talking about the center. 'Things fall apart, the center cannot hold.' Or, in the case of physics, the whole lot of formless matter—molecules, atoms, and those items that came before our own universe was formed. You remember the laws of thermodynamics, don't you?"

Jeez! Those laws again. Did those laws apply to everything in the whole universe? The laws looked simple, but weren't: 1) Everything is made of stuff, like molecules and atoms. 2) The stuff is moving all the time. 3) The stuff falls apart.

Whoa! The stuff falls apart! I sort of began to get it.

"These laws apply to everything in the whole universe," said Althea. "Even this poem. You could read this poem just like a physics lesson. The laws of thermodynamics explain how molecules and atoms stick together. If they didn't stick together, we wouldn't be here. Without order, everything is confused. A mess. This poem is saying the same thing. Without the rules of civilized behavior—a sort of human chaos results. He's saying chaos is formed when people don't follow the rules. People become rough beasts. They become cruel. Angry. Hateful."

"So what are the people laws?"

"Treat others the way you want to be treated. That about covers everything."

Now this didn't seem right to me. I mean, what if you are a crazy person? In New York City, where my family lives, when Mom and Dad aren't off somewhere on business, there are people who stand in front of your car when you're going down the street and make you give them money to wash your perfectly clean windshield. If you don't, they'll like, smash your car or whatever. And what about, like, a drug addict. Drug addicts want to do drugs. "If everybody went around treating others the way they wanted to be treated, you'd have a big mess," I said. "Everybody wants to be treated different."

"Everybody wants to be warm, to have enough to eat, and someone to love them," Althea said. "I think, myself, that when you see people behaving badly, it's because they've made a whole bunch of bad choices up front. And what you see when you see people being awful is people trying to get back to being warm, fed, and loved."

I wasn't sure about this. People like Jeff Loomis wanted to be loved? I don't *think* so. "I think Jeff Loomis wants to be hated. He called Amanda Saadiq a nigger," I said.

Althea looked very very angry. "He did? When?"

"This morning. And Jeff Loomis's father has so much money, Jeff can eat whatever he wants sixty times a day. And you should see the money his mother spends on sweaters for him and for Brett. Jeff's warm, fed, and loved all right. And he doesn't even deserve it."

"Do you think anyone really loves Jeff Loomis?"

"His father must," I said. "Look at all the stuff he gives Jeff and Brett."

Althea sighed. "Getting material things is not what love is really about, Natalie. And as for Jeff and his hateful behavior, well . . . There's as much wickedness in the world as good. A lot of the times wickedness and good are mixed up in the same person. The choices you make every day have a lot to do with how you turn out. Does *that* help you at all?"

No, it did not. This was all blah. I was absolutely going to have to figure this whole magic thing out for myself. I could see that right now.

"All right, Natalie. Let's try this. Jeff called Amanda a truly hateful name. You clearly want to do something about it. What can you do?"

I did *not* want to talk about this. I knew what I'd done about it. I'd run right off. I hadn't done a thing.

"I don't know," I mumbled like a true dweeb. I knew Althea wouldn't be all hot on what I wanted to answer: push Jeff Loomis into the nearest manure pile. Or call him a zillion different kinds of a dork. Althea wasn't much on what she called "violence as a solution."

"Why don't you like Jeff?"

"He thinks he so hot. And he's mean."

"And he doesn't respect you."

"No."

"And he doesn't respect Amanda. Clearly."

"No."

"Do you deserve respect?"

"Well, sure. I guess."

"You do," said Althea firmly. "Does Amanda deserve respect?"

"Yeah!"

"Why?"

"She's the best rider I've ever seen! She loves that horse. And that horse loves her. And you can see it when they ride."

"She also has a lot of talent," said Althea. "When the two of them are in the arena together . . . it's beautiful."

"It makes me want to cry," I admitted in a low voice.

Althea smiled. "Me, too. I respect that. I respect Amanda."

"And I don't respect Jeff," I said. A sudden, horrible idea hit me. If these people laws were like the laws of thermodynamics, did that mean I had to like, respect Jeff Loomis?! Would everything fall apart if I didn't treat him like I wanted to be treated? Aaaggh!

"Jeff hasn't earned your respect," Althea said, like she was reading my mind. "And you *don't* have to give it to him. That's what you can do about what he called Amanda. That means if he says lousy things— who cares? He's not worthy of respect. He hasn't earned it. Amanda's earned it." Althea started waving her arms around. I had no idea she could get this excited about these people laws. "Bart deserves it! So do your mother and father. And John Ironheels! And you! And me!"

I hated to do this. I mean, Althea was having a great old time, and I could definitely see what she was saying about how respect is this big deal. But I had to. I mean, the way it was turning out, Jeff Loomis was a lot like this beast that showed up when I got greedy or mean. Was this beast going to disappear if I said, "Beat it, you don't have my respect!" into its no-face? I don't *think* so. So I really had to know what else I could do to keep the beast from getting Denny, if that's what it was after. I tugged at Althea's T-shirt. She was still hollering about the people you respect and the people you don't. *"How do I stop him?"*

Althea stopped with her arms in midair. "Stop who?"

"The be—I mean, Jeff Loomis. I mean, it doesn't do any good just to go around not respecting him. He's such a jerk he won't even notice. And besides . . ." I trailed off. The beast wings had darkened the light. Its wings had been cold. Mindy had been terrified of it. And me—I was terrified, too. And Denny. What if it was really after Denny? "I don't know *what* to do."

"Sometimes, Natalie, the only thing to do is stand up for yourself and what you know is true. You take action. Even though it might be a little embarrassing. I think the first thing to do is to refuse to take part. Nicely, of course. But when Jeff called Amanda what he did, you might say something like, please don't use that word in front of me. And if he challenges you, just walk away."

"What if he keeps on doing it?"

"In that case"—Althea gave me a hug—"you call

in a higher authority. The law. Like me. Or your parents. Or Bart."

Ha! The law. Suleiman had talked about the Law, too. Things were beginning to make a little more sense: Althea didn't know it, but she was talking about the Law of the Turtle.

# CHAPTER

## ELEVEN

I HUNG OVER THE FENCE AND WATCHED SULEIMAN the Magnificent grazing. Stillmeadow Farm was quiet. The roses from Uncle Bart's flower bed smelled sweet. All the people who had been here for the riding lessons had gone home. Denny and I had a tutoring session with Althea, so that was done for the day. I'd finished my share of afternoon chores, too, which was mucking out four stalls. Mucking out is when you scoop all the manure and horse pee out of the stall the horse has been in. Then you dump in fresh wood shavings for bedding. The scooping part is a pain, but I like dumping the wood shavings. They smell fresh and clean. You have to make the bedding pretty deep, so the horse is comfy when it lies down to sleep at night. So I'd hauled a lot of loads of shavings in the wheelbarrow. I was pretty tired. The sun was hot—but a real nice breeze took care of my sweat. It was four o'clock; all the horses who had been turned out in the pasture for the day would be coming in for evening feed.

"Did you have a good day, boy?" I said to Suleiman the Magnificent. He flicked his ear, but kept his muzzle close to the grass. You have to be careful about how much grass horses get in spring. When the pasture's new and the grass is that bright green that only comes in early June, the horse can eat so much it will get the colic and die. Or maybe it will "founder" and die. Colic is a terrible stomachache, where the horse's stomach fills up with gas from eating too much. Horses aren't like people; when horses get gas in their stomachs, it can get so huge it will stop their hearts and burst their stomachs. Founder is from eating too much green grass, too. Founder is when the grass sends all the blood to the horse's feet. Uncle Bart says it is just like hitting your own thumbnail with a hammer, only the horse has to walk on its feet and you don't have to walk on your thumbs.

I watched Suleiman the Magnificent for any signs of founder or colic. But I knew Amanda took such good care of him that there wasn't much hope of saving him from colic and like that.

And there wasn't much hope of me and Mindy Blue entering the Olympics, either.

"I've decided about the magic," I said to Suleiman. He flicked the other ear. "I'm only going to use it when people need respect."

He raised his head and looked at me. His eyelids wrinkled up in this real nice way horses have when they are asking you a question.

"Animals, too," I said, in case his feelings were

hurt. "It's because of the beast, and all. And the laws."

Suleiman seemed to nod, although I know he didn't, not really. Without Denny and the pearl necklace, he couldn't understand me at all. Or at least, just in the way all horses understand people.

"Here, boy," I said, and held out a carrot. Suleiman walked over like the king he was. Head high, neck arched, silky tail flowing long and graceful in the wind. He took the carrot like a present you don't want to seem too greedy for.

"He's proud," Amanda Saadiq said. I twisted my head around and then jumped off the fence. She'd changed out of her riding breeches and was wearing jeans and a bright shirt. Her head was wrapped in a cotton scarf. Her neck looked long and proud, like the stallion's.

The thing about older girls is this. The juniors and seniors at my high school are kind of stuck-up about thirteen-year-old kids like me. So you don't, like, try and hang out with them or anything. "I was just saying hi," I said. "Uncle Bart will be here to take him in soon."

Amanda swung her right hand up with a smile. She was carrying a red lead line. "I'll take him in."

I, like, really wanted to help put Suleiman in his stall. There were certain horses I was not allowed to handle at Stillmeadow. Uncle Bart's own personal horse, Moonshadow, of course, and any stallion or boarder's horse. I'd never even been on the same side of the fence with Suleiman. There's a lot to do when you take a horse in from pasture. But I wasn't all that sure Amanda wanted me around. Besides, there's a lot of times when I want to be alone with Mindy Blue. Maybe Amanda wanted to be alone with Suleiman. I kind of shifted from one foot to the other and felt like a total dweeb.

Amanda glanced at me. She had a soft, slow way of moving. "Want to help?"

Did I!

"You stand the gate," said Amanda. So I opened the gate for her and held it closed while she went up to Suleiman. She approached him from the side, since horses don't like you to go at them head-on. She made a soft shushing sound like "ssshewy shhweey," and he bent his head so she could snap the lead line on his halter, under his chin. I waited until she was near the gate with him, just in case he decided to run out on his own, then swung it wide again. I closed it and latched it after they went through, and then just kind of stood there. You never really know if older girls mean it when they say they want you around.

"Would you like to walk along with us?" asked Amanda.

I wanted to jump up and down, but I didn't. You never jump around horses, even the ones you know really well, like Mindy Blue. So I did like Amanda, and tried to move soft and slow. All three of us walked together into the barn, which was dark and cool after the sunshine outside.

Suleiman had his own special stall, away from the other horses. This was because he was a stallion. When the mares in the barn come into heat, a stallion gets restless, wanting to go to them to breed the mares so that there would be baby foals in the spring. When a stallion gets restless, he stamps his feet and kicks the stall with his powerful hooves. He snorts and bellows and makes a lot of noise. Stallions get bossy with the geldings sometimes, too, since they are used to being kings of the herd. So any stallion in Uncle Bart's barn has his own stall, away from the others. Otherwise, there may be a ruckus.

We took Suleiman down the concrete aisle of the big barn. I hadn't realized how big he was until I was walking alongside of him and Amanda. Horses are measured by what's called a "hand," which is four inches. You measure the number of hands from the top of the horse's shoulders to the ground.

"He's really big," I said to Amanda as we walked along, just like we were both in charge of this horse. "More than sixteen hands, I bet."

"He's close to seventeen," she said. "He's sixteen hands and three inches."

It took me a second to figure this out, but I'm pretty good at multiplying in my head. Suleiman was sixty-seven inches tall, so it was just a little short of six feet from the top of his shoulder to the ground. No wonder I felt like a dwarf.

Suleiman sort of rumbled at each of the horses as we passed them in their stalls. They were all looking at him with their ears up and their eyes bright. Most of them would wait until he was past their stall. Then they would whinny a little bit in sort of a salute.

Amanda stopped him in front of his stall and put him in the cross ties. Cross ties are ropes with snaps at the end. One end of the rope is attached to the barn ceiling with bolts. The other snaps on to the horse's halter. The ropes are at right angles to where the horse stands, so there is one for the left side and one for the right. Suleiman stood quietly in the cross ties.

Amanda smiled at me. "Would you like to take off his leg wraps, Natalie? I'll get the brushes."

Would I! I bent down and carefully unwound the soft cloth wraps around his forelegs. Suleiman was always turned out in leg wraps so he wouldn't bruise himself in the pasture. Amanda brought the grooming kit and gave me a currycomb. A currycomb is a rubber pad with soft points on the bottom. When you curry a horse, you scrub the currycomb in a circular motion all over the horse's hide.

"Put your back into it," said Amanda in a nice way.

I worked up a real sweat currying that horse. He really seemed to like it. I curried his left side and neck and belly, and Amanda curried his right. All the while we were currying, Amanda talked to him in a low singing voice, like water in a meadow's brook.

We curried until every speck of his silver hide was standing up like little pieces of grass. Then Amanda gave me a brush. We brushed and brushed until all the hair on his coat was flat and smooth. Finally we each took a polishing cloth and wiped him down.

Amanda got water from the barn pump and she washed his ears, nose, and dock. The dock is the part of the horse under the tail, and Suleiman grumbled a bit when she did that. I combed out his mane and tail.

"We just need to pick out his feet and then we can feed him, Natalie." She stood at his head, facing his tail. Then she bent down and pinched his ankle very lightly. He picked up his hoof right away. When you try this with Denny's pony, Susie, she doesn't pick up her foot at all. Instead, she leans on you just like you were a post. Susie has terrible barn manners. It was a good thing Suleiman had good barn manners. He must have weighed fourteen hundred pounds with all the muscle on him. If he leaned on Amanda, she'd be squashed flat.

Amanda tucked his foot between her knees and scooped out all the dirt in his hooves with a plastic pick. I handed her a little brush just made for horse hooves, and she brushed out all the little bits of gravel and everything. She picked out each of his feet. Then he sighed like, "So, *that's* finished," and we patted him and put him in his stall.

His grain was already in his bin, and the hayrack was full. I looked in his water bucket. Either Uncle Bart or Althea had already scrubbed it out, and it was filled with fresh clear water. Amanda and I leaned against the stall door and watched him eat. He didn't stick his nose into his grain bin and chomp away like other horses did. He ate a few bits of oats, then raised his head and looked around. Then he'd eat a few more.

"He's very alert," said Amanda, "like most stallions."

"He's the most beautiful horse I've ever seen," I said. "Did your mom and dad buy him for you?"

"You crazy, girl?" Amanda laughed, but not in a

rude way. "This horse is worth thousands of dollars. There's no way my parents could afford him. No. Suleiman belongs to the company my dad works for. The Girodani Cheese Company."

"Suleiman belongs to people who make cheese?"

"Well, yes. They sponsored me on the A-circuit last year. And if I make the team, for the Olympics."

I thought of Jeff Loomis. Maybe he wasn't just blabbering when he said his father was going to buy Suleiman. I mean, if Suleiman was my horse, I'd be dead in a ditch before I sold him to anybody, much less the horrible Loomis kids. But if Suleiman belonged to your father's boss . . .

"I thought he was yours!" I blurted out.

Amanda was quiet for a long long minute. Then: "His heart, Natalie, his heart is mine."

A shadow darkened the window in Suleiman's stall. For one second I was sure the shadowy beast was back. I blinked hard, confused and a little scared. Something weird was going on!

"Amanda?"

Phew! It was just Uncle Bart and some other guys with him. Suleiman reared a little and snorted—a harsh, loud sound that meant, "Stay away!" Uncle Bart walked into the barn and up to Suleiman's stall. I recognized one of the two men with him: it was Mr. Loomis. I didn't know the other man, but Amanda did. She stood even straighter than she had before. She got that extra-polite look on her face, the one she used when we met for the first time; like she was *there,* in person, but her heart was far away. She nodded politely at this other man. He was tall and skinny, and he had black hair. He was pale, like he never got outside. "How are you, Mr. Girodani? Natalie, this is my father's boss. Sir? I'd like you to meet my friend Natalie Ross."

"I know the little lady," Mr. Loomis boomed. He sort of shouldered Mr. Girodani out of the way. Now, sometimes adults will say to me or Denny in this shrieky voice, "Ooo, you look just like your father." Or, "My goodness! Doesn't she have her mother's nose," which is uncool, but okay, since I really like the way Mom and Dad look. Nobody would say Jeff or Brett looked anything like their dad, which was the only good thing in the known universe about Jeff and Brett. Mr. Loomis was a tall person with a fat stomach, red face, and little beady eyes. In my opinion, he looked like a big mean pig, but you can't say that aloud about adults, of course, even in the middle of the worst temper tantrum in the world.

Mr. Loomis grabbed at me for a hug and, when I ducked, pinched my cheek instead. It hurt. "Giro-dani, this little blond cutie is Bart's niece. And if you think she's a little beauty, you ought to see her mother." He smacked his big rubbery lips.

It was just, like—*gag!* I just, like, *looked* at Amanda. She rolled her eyes ever so slightly at me. Without even thinking about it, we moved closer together.

"I'm Albert Girodani, Natalie," said the other man. "I see you've been admiring my horse." He kind of tippy-toed into Suleiman's stall. The big horse pawed at the floor and blew out, a warning signal. "Hey!" said Mr. Girodani. "Settle down!" Then he hit Suleiman in the shoulder. Suleiman jerked back. "You gotta teach a horse who's boss right off the bat, Loomis," he said over his shoulder. He turned back to the stallion. "Right, big boy?" He smacked Suleiman on the chest, hard. Suleiman stretched his neck straight out, raised his head, and bared his teeth.

Uncle Bart cleared his throat in a warning way. When a stallion rolls his lips back over his teeth, he is saying that he is going to take action. Mr. Girodani must have known it, too, because he jumped out of that stall like he was standing in fire. Suleiman reared and whinnied like a bugle.

Again, without even so much as a nudge between us, Amanda and I acted like a team. She went to Suleiman's head, and reached up and stroked his nose. I took his halter from the other side and patted his flank. We both went, "Easy, boy, easy," since it was clear as water that Suleiman didn't think too much of Mr. Girodani.

"Full of spirit," said Mr. Girodani, a little nervously. "What in blazes have you been doing to this horse, Amanda?"

"We interrupted Suleiman's dinner," said Uncle Bart in a too-loud, too-jokey voice. "Gentlemen, why don't we go on up to the house for some coffee?"

"Heck, no." Mr. Girodani scowled. "I want Loomis here to see the son of a gun work in the arena. Amanda? Tack him up."

"Right now?" said Amanda, startled.

"Right now. Go on, move it."

"Well, I . . ." She got even quieter. More distant. "Certainly, Mr. Girodani."

"I'll help," I said.

"Natalie . . ." Uncle Bart started to say. Then: "Never mind. Fine. We'll see you two in the arena."

"Ten minutes," said Amanda. "I'll change into my riding gear."

"Ten minutes," said Uncle Bart.

They went away.

"Can't they even let Suleiman eat?" I said. I was mad. "What a bunch of jerks."

"Shhh," said Amanda. "It's Mr. Girodani's horse, remember."

Suleiman nudged his head against her chest.

"Why does he want to see him now?" I said. "Why can't they wait until the schooling class tomorrow?"

"Maybe he's just showing off to Mr. Loomis." Amanda clipped the lead line under Suleiman's chin and led him into the aisle. "Can you get the Passier saddle for me, Natalie? And the thin horse pad, not the thick one. I'll just go into this stall and change into my breeches."

I got the saddle for her, and the double bridle. We brushed Suleiman smooth one more time, then tacked him up. Suleiman was patient, only nudging Amanda with his nose once or twice. When she ducked under his head to adjust the breastplate, he rested his nose in her hair and blew softly into it.

The sun was going down as we walked out of the big barn to the arena. It was still light—and would be for another couple of hours—but the moon rode high and white in the wisps of clouds on the horizon. Uncle Bart had turned the lights on in the arena.

When we walked in, the whole place was lit up like for a show.

Uncle Bart's arena was set up for dressage and jumping. Stillmeadow Farms' specialty was training horses for three-day events—which a lot of people say is the best test of a horse and rider. In three-day eventing, the horse and rider spend one day at stadium jumping, which is basically going over hurdles insides a big arena, one day at cross-country, which is jumping horses over hedges and fences outside, and one day at dressage. Uncle Bart says that dressage is the ultimate test of a rider's ability to communicate with the horse. Dressage is when the rider seems to sit perfectly still, and the horse does these beautiful dancey movements all over the arena: dancey movements like pirouettes, curvettes, and the levade, which is a controlled leap with all four feet off the ground. Good dressage will make even the toughest person cry at the beauty if they know what they are looking at.

Uncle Bart says that people who don't know horses very well think jumping high is the best thing to watch—but it isn't true. Jumping is fun. Dressage is like, art. Art to the max.

"Let's see 'im jump!" roared Mr. Loomis as Amanda and I took Suleiman into the arena. He was sitting up in the stands with Mr. Girodani and Uncle Bart. I squinted into the bright lights. Althea was there and so was the glaring red that was Denny's hair. So the rest of him must've been there, too, but I couldn't see too well on account of the arena lights. But I could see who sat behind Denny: Brett Loomis and the horrible Jeff. Far up in the bleacher I saw John Ironheels, or at least his hat and his fringed suede jacket.

The sand arena had mirrors along the side so that a person could see how they looked when they were riding. There were eight jumps set in a figure eight in the middle. Suleiman took a look at the jumps, arched his neck, and whinnied.

"Get a move on, Amanda," shouted Mr. Girodani. "If the animal's giving you any trouble, give it the whip."

Amanda's shoulders stiffened. I reached out and patted her arm. She gave me a tight smile. "No use to get mad," my look said.

"He's a *jerk,*" her look said back.

I gave her a leg up. A leg up is when you help a rider into the saddle. You stand by the horse, crouch down a little, and cup your hands. The rider puts the left leg in the stirrup iron and leaps off the ground with the right. As the rider leaps, the right knee comes into your cupped hands and you push up. If you do it right, if you do it like a team, giving a leg up is as smooth as smooth. The rider's weight never hits your hands at all.

I gave Amanda a leg up as smooth as smooth.

We were a team.

She settled into the saddle and gave me a wink. I gave her a secret thumbs-up. Then I went to the bleachers to sit with Althea and Denny. Althea gave me a worried little smile. Denny crossed his eyes at me, grinned, stuck his tongue out, and generally goofed off like he usually does. Behind me, Jeff and

Brett whispered and giggled. The arena spread out before me, seeming bigger than it usually did. Amanda looked very small on the giant horse.

"Get a move on," shouted Mr. Girodani at Amanda.

They started out at an uncollected walk, just loosening up. "Collected" means that all the muscles of the horse are tightened up and ready to work. You collect a horse slowly, giving it a chance to fall into the rhythm of the gaits. Mr. Girodani started yelling right away, "Go on! Move it on out!" and yodeling "whup-whup-whup" and like that. Jeff Loomis joined in, then his piggy father. I was, like, totally amazed that Amanda was unflapped. She and Suleiman ignored them all. She circled the ring once at an uncollected walk, Then she drew the reins up ever so slightly, straightened her back, and—although you couldn't see it, because it was so smooth, so quiet—she tightened her legs, drove her bottom lightly into the saddle, and Suleiman moved into a collected trot like a leaf on water.

He was light. He floated. His neck was arched and his beautiful silky nose was tucked into his chest. His legs moved with elegance and in perfect rhythm.

"Oh, come on!" yelled Mr. Loomis. "For the Lord's sake, jump!"

"They're set at two-six, Amanda," said Uncle Bart. He didn't need to yell like some fat-faced people; his voice carried across the arena just as clear as if he had been standing right next to me.

Amanda nodded, just a little, and Suleiman swung a tight circle and moved into a quiet canter. A two-six is a jump two feet six inches high. That doesn't sound very high—it's even shorter than Denny—but you'd be amazed at how high two-six can seem on a horse—even one as big as Suleiman. He took that two-six like he was puddle-jumping, and the one after that and the one after that. Althea grabbed my hand and squeezed it. I squeezed back. I wanted to cheer.

"Higher," shouted Kevin, "put the jumps higher!"

Amanda put Suleiman into a halt, facing Jeff and his father. "He worked hard today," she said softly. "Hard and well. He deserves a rest. I'm afraid, Mr. Girodani, that it will undo what he learned today, if we push."

"Don't get uppity with me, girl," said Mr. Girodani between his teeth. "Get on with it."

I got that creepy feeling you get when adults are talking about stuff like sex, and like that. Stuff that you aren't supposed to understand, and if you do, you'd be so embarrassed that you'd die right there on the spot.

Althea jerked her hand out of mine, turned, and glared at Mr. Girodani. I felt her take a deep breath. Uncle Bart, who was sitting just beyond Mr. Girodani, leaned back and sent Althea a look. It was a warning look, if I ever saw one. He shook his head, ever so slightly. Althea's voice was calm. When she spoke, there was just a little shake in it. "I'm sure you didn't mean that like it sounded, Mr. Girodani."

"Like what?" Denny demanded. "What did it sound like?"

"Rude," said Althea flatly, "and insulting."

Mr. Girodani turned red. "That's *my horse*," he said.

"And Amanda's our friend," said Uncle Bart. "We have a rule in this barn, Mr. Girodani. And the bottom line is respect. For everyone."

In the arena, Amanda was cooling Suleiman out. Cooling out is when you get off the horse and walk it around and around until the sweat the horse has worked up is gone.

"She got off, Dad," said Jeff Loomis. "And all she did was take him over those piddly little jumps."

"I'd like to see *you* go over those piddly little jumps," I said. Althea frowned at me.

"Well, just maybe I will," said Jeff.

"Just maybe you won't," I said. "Just maybe—" Althea gave me a sharp nudge. I sat back and shut up.

"It's not a bad idea," said Mr. Loomis. "Jeff'll show her a thing or two. Go on, Jeff."

I turned around and gave Jeff a big fat smirk. There was no way Jeff Loomis could ride Suleiman. Not in ten million years. The horse was too big and powerful. Only a top rider could handle him. I could tell from looking at him that Jeff knew it, too.

"Maybe she's right, Dad," said Jeff. "Amanda rode the horse into the ground today. I'll ride him tomorrow."

"Now, son," said Mr. Loomis.

There was a nasty feeling in the air again. Mr. Loomis was glaring at Jeff like, "You coward, you." Mr. Girodani was smirking away, like, "Who do you think *your* kid is, Loomis?"

"Get on the horse, Jeff," said Mr. Loomis.

"Bart?" said Althea in a worried tone.

"It'll be all right. Just take it easy, Jeff," said Uncle Bart. "You'll handle the gaits just fine. Take him around at a walk then a trot, then leave—"

"He'll take the jumps," said Mr. Loomis. "And he'll take them now."

"All *right*!"

Jeff slammed down the bleachers to the arena. Suleiman jerked back when he walked up to Amanda. She hesitated. Looked up at me.

"Get on the damn horse!" Mr. Loomis hollered. "I'm not going to buy you the damn thing if you don't ride it, Jeff."

Amanda's face turned from its beautiful brown to a milky coffee color. Her body jerked, like she'd been shot. She hadn't known, I thought. Oh, no. She hadn't known that Jeff was going to buy this horse.

"Steady, Amanda," I heard Althea whisper beside me. "Steady."

There was something hot at my neck. I slapped my hand against my chest. The pearl necklace blazed like fire. I cupped the pearl in my hand so Althea couldn't see, and drew it out from under my T-shirt to look at it. It was glowing with red, angry light.

"Denny," I said in a low voice, "Denny. C'mon. We've got work to do."

# CHAPTER

## Twelve

"YOU GUYS ARE LEAVING?" ALTHEA ASKED.

"Be right back!" I promised. "Come *on,* Denny." I grabbed him by the T-shirt and practically dragged him out of the arena. Sitting there, watching that beautiful Amanda and that awesome horse take all that rotten stuff from the Loomises, I'd decided to use the magic. Amanda had worked day after day, month after month, year after year to get as good as she was. And it wasn't going to be wrecked by some bigoted bozos. I thought about Amanda pushing wheelbarrows full of horse manure through a blizzard twice a day in the wintertime. It was hard enough pushing wheelbarrows full of horse manure in the summertime.

My dreams about the Olympics? Well, how would I feel winning the Olympic Gold Medal, knowing I'd won by magic? How would I feel getting *anything* by magic?

For just a second I was sorry I wasn't going to save the magic for myself. "Darn it," I said. There were so many things it'd be cool to use the magic for: getting A's in geometry without studying; having Brian Kurlander ask me to the junior prom next year instead of that icky Vicky Birdsell, who had practically perfect hair. But then, once I used it, I'd have to go *on* using the magic. If I never did anything on my own, the magic would trap me. I'd be, like, a slave to it for the rest of my life. I'd never just be me, Natalie Carmichael Ross, getting A's and beating out Vicky Birdsell and all that.

There was a small side door to Uncle Bart's office. I pushed Denny in there, leaving it open a crack so we could see out.

"What are you doing to me?" he hollered. "Nata—"

I stuck my hand over his mouth. He sort of sighed and looked up at me over my hand. I took my hand away. Then I wiped it on my jeans because my palm was full of Denny-drool. I didn't holler back at him, though. It seemed like one way or the other, I was always trying to shut poor old Denny up. Here I was all mad about the way Jeff Loomis and his horrible pig-parent were treating Amanda; maybe I wasn't treating Denny all that hot either. I mean, the poor kid hadn't asked to be a wizard, had he? And he couldn't even remember it when he wasn't full of it— the magic, I mean. If the two of us were going to use this magic, it had to be together. Like Amanda and me. A team.

Also, we had to use it for other people, instead of,

well, me. Otherwise, that beast might turn right around and head toward Cayuga Lake instead of the Middle East.

Jeez. Partners with a six-year-old whose entire mission in life was, like, to drive me berserker bananas. On the other hand—life could be worse. I was excited: this was my first official use of the magic in the right way. I wondered if I should say something nice to the turtle, first. "Thanks, sir," I said. "We'll try to do right by the necklace."

I was ready. I bent down and looked Denny straight in the eye. I tried to sound unflapped, like Amanda. "Okay, Dennis. We're going to do something totally cool. Are you ready?"

He looked suspicious. "What?" he said. Then he started to belch. *Bur-wurp! Bur-wurp!* This was Denny's latest thing, that he could belch. This made me mad. I mean, here I was, like, reformed and everything, and this magic was serious stuff, and the kid didn't even appreciate it.

"Stop it, Denny. I'm serious. Do you want Jeff Loomis and his father to have Suleiman?"

Denny scowled. "No!"

"What would Spiderman do?"

Denny made a fist, swept it in the air, and yelled, "Ka-*pow*! Right in the kisser!"

I heard shouts from the arena. I looked over my shoulder. Jeff was riding Suleiman around the arena at a fast, sloppy trot. You could tell the horse was upset. His ears were pinned back. He had his head stretched out and foam was flying from his lips where he was working the bit. Jeff was bouncing along on his back on the wrong diagonal. For a horse as sensitive as Suleiman, this is torture. The only good thing about it was that it was torture for Jeff, too.

"Not ka-pow right in the kisser, Denny." I took his hand. "If Spiderman had it, he would use it. Magic."

"Magic."

I drew the pearl necklace over my head. The fiery red was gone. The pearl was glowing with soft pink light. I held the necklace out with one hand and held on to Denny with the other. His eyes began to glow with magical green. The oceany mist of the pearl rose about us, like clouds rising from the earth itself. We turned, the two of us—

*three of us*, came the vast, kind Voice of the Turtle.

—to the arena. Suleiman was racing now, his eyes rolled back in his head. White foam came from his mouth. Jeff was on his back, sawing away at the reins to stop him.

"Give 'im the whip!" Mr. Loomis shouted. "You damn-fool kid!"

The mist of the pearl made me see things I couldn't see before. I saw tears in Amanda's eyes. I heard the angry beating of Althea's heart. I felt Uncle Bart gritting his teeth, and clenching and unclenching his fists, like he wanted to hit somebody.

"Make him sleepy, Denny," I whispered in the warmth of the pearl sea. "Make Suleiman sleepy."

Green fire trickled from Denny's fingers like syrup out of a bottle. It flowed sweet as sweet, right through the air around Suleiman's head and ears.

"Hush, now," I half sang. "Hush, boy."

Well, you would have thought that good old horse hadn't had a nap for days. He slowed down. Stopped. Then he yawned a giant yawn, his pink tongue sticking out between his big white teeth.

"Hey!" Jeff yelled. He was so surprised he stopped sawing away on the reins.

Suleiman yawned again. Then he stretched, ahead and behind, just like good old Bunkie before she goes to sleep at night.

"Great, Denny," I said, real low. I knew no one could see the magic except Denny and me, but I was pretty sure we could be heard, even if we were floating in this pale pearl sea. "That's great!"

Suleiman locked his knees and closed his eyes. Horses have this special joint in their kneebones that lets them do this, so they don't fall over when they go to sleep. On top of him, Jeff was banging away with his heels, but good old Suleiman just snoozed away. It was terrific.

Well, there was a bunch of hollering at that. Uncle Bart came running up with Althea close behind. Amanda ran to Suleiman's head and stroked his nose. She whispered in his ear, her face tight and worried.

Jeff jumped off the sleeping horse in total disgust and stalked off like somebody finally told him what a dork he was. Somebody else said, "We'll have to call the vet." I decided it was time we woke good old Suleiman right up, or there'd be some weird explaining to do.

"Okay, Denny. Wake him up."

Denny curled his fingers closed and the soft green

magic stopped. Only it stopped quicker than we thought. Good old Suleiman woke up right in the middle of a snore. He saw all this people crowding around him and reared up with a good old whinny that about half took the roof off. Uncle Bart and Althea jumped out of the way. Like Uncle Bart says, you're always going to lose a war with something that's bigger than you are. Mr. Loomis, who was poking the horse in this very rude way, fell right over on his butt, which was the coolest thing I'd seen in a while.

I let go of Denny's hand. The pink sea swirled away, just like water down the shower drain. The pearl necklace was its ordinary color—cool and white. I slipped it over my neck. Then Denny and I came out of Uncle Bart's office and walked into the arena.

I felt terrific. I didn't feel the slightest of bit of worry that the beast was hanging around. So it must have been a good use of the magic.

"Do you think I should call the vet, Mr. Carmichael?" Amanda stepped back and looked at Suleiman from head to tail. Without the help of the magic, I couldn't tell if she was crying inside or not. There was a little crease of worry on her forehead, though. "He *seems* okay. But it was so weird, his falling asleep like that."

Uncle Bart ran his hands down Suleiman's legs, then put his ear to the horse's belly and listened. "Doesn't seem to be a thing wrong with him that I can see."

John Ironheels touched my arm. He winked at me,

in such a quiet way that nobody noticed. "I think the horse will be fine, Bart," he said.

"Fine? What the *hell* do you mean, fine?" yelled Mr. Girodani. "What the *devil* have you done to my horse, girl?" He glared at Amanda.

"I'm as baffled at you are, sir," Amanda said. She was just as cool as cool.

"It might be a little premature to think about selling the stallion, though," said Uncle Bart.

"You're darn straight about that, Carmichael." Mr. Loomis puffed. Hooray! The Loomises weren't going to buy Suleiman. I decided he didn't look as much like a pig as I'd thought. More like a big dumb turkey.

"It's no wonder my boy Jeff had such trouble with that fool animal. And you, Girodani . . ." He swung around and stuck his finger practically in Mr. Girodani's face. "You'd better get yourself another rider. That little colored girl you've got is going to lose you a pile of money. Mark my words."

Fire Amanda? Mr. Loomis was back to looking like a pig again.

Even without the magic, I could tell that Uncle Bart wanted to smack Mr. Loomis right in the kisser. Althea put her hand on Uncle Bart's arm in a soothing kind of way. "Amanda's an African-American, Mr. Loomis. If you feel absolutely compelled to refer to her race, you'll refer to her that way, please." It was her no-nonsense, firm, do-it-my-way tutor voice. "Bart used the word 'respect.' I'm going to use it again. If you can't respect us—any of us—there's no room for you or your horses at Stillmeadow Farm."

Mr. Loomis went "Ha!" then, "C'mon, Jeff." They walked right off without even so much as a good-bye. Brett scuttled after them.

"Good riddance," said Althea loudly.

"That don't solve my problem," said Mr. Girodani. He rubbed his hands over his face and sighed. "Bart? I took a chance when I listened to you about how Amanda's color wasn't going to make a difference."

"It hasn't," said Uncle Bart in this clipped, angry way. "I mean she's taken every prize on the A-circuit."

"The Olympics are different. Amanda—you're one heck of a rider. I don't care what happened tonight, that horse is good. And you're even better. But Loomis is right. I can't think of one col—I mean African-American rider on the whole East Coast circuit. Can you?"

Amanda looked at her boots. She was breathing hard and trying not to show it.

"Mr. Girodani," said Uncle Bart. "Amanda's race doesn't have a thing to do with her talent. I told you that before you decided to recruit her to ride Suleiman, and I'm telling you now."

"Sorry, Bart, but it does. You think of one African-American who's won a Gold Medal in the equestrian events, one African-American who's won big on the A-circuit except for her—then I'll reconsider. I—and my company—well, we've sunk a lot of money into this project. I don't think I can risk any more."

"You're not considering taking Suleiman out of the qualifying trials?" Uncle Bart asked.

"Not Suleiman, no. But Amanda, yes." He walked

over to where Amanda was standing. "I've got a couple of riders in mind who could take over. You listen to me, Amanda. It doesn't make any difference to me whether you're green, yellow, purple, or black. And Loomis is a jerk. You won't find any disagreement from me there. But he's a jerk who's right. I can't risk it. You just don't see people of your color in the big-time horse shows."

Amanda raised her head. Her dark eyes were shining with fury. Her lips were drawn tight. But her voice was low and even. "I've heard that before—it doesn't matter to me, you said. Whether I'm black or green or purple, you said. But it does matter, Mr. Girodani. It does matter. Because you're pulling me out of the show."

Mr. Girodani raised his hands. "Now, I haven't said that for sure. You just give me a couple of days to think about it."

"What about the trials?" asked Bart. "The trials are tomorrow. You can't just throw any rider on that stallion. You're asking for a huge train wreck."

"That so?" Mr. Girodani frowned. "But the horse and rider both have to qualify, right? You can ride him in the trials, Amanda. But no further. I gotta get a new pro."

"That's not fair!" Althea burst out. "That's absolutely ridiculous. There's some prejudice on the circuit, sure. But it's not everywhere. And the judge we have tomorrow has an excellent reputation."

"Sorry, Althea, Bart. I just can't risk it. There's too much money at stake for me and my company."

Uncle Bart's voice was quiet but firm. "Don't apologize to me, Mr. Girodani. It's Amanda who deserves the apology. She's worked hard on this horse. If you'd seen her work here this year . . ." He stopped and shook his head. "She was here every day, in ten-degree cold and ninety-degree heat. In blizzards and torrential storms. I've never seen such dedication. And I'll tell you something else. I'm not a sentimental man—but that horse loves her. She'll get the best out of him—because she has his heart."

Mr. Girodani shook his head. "I hear you. I hear you, Bart. But Al Girodani's an executive, and I make executive decisions." He clapped his hand on Amanda's shoulder. "Now—I can't be here tomorrow—so we'll let those judges decide, okay? You win or you're done as a Girodani rider. Sorry, kid."

Amanda didn't flinch. Not one little bit. We all watched Mr. Girodani walk across the arena and out the door.

"It's not fair!" Denny yelled, which surprised me a lot. I didn't even think he knew what was going on. "You're the best!"

Amanda looked at me. That faraway look was in her eye—like she was here, but not with us. "That's the problem, you know. I can't be ordinary. I can't be average. I have to be better than everyone else—just to get in." She turned to the horse. "The only being my color doesn't matter to is him."

"It doesn't matter to me," I said.

"Or to me," Althea said. "Or to Bart or John, or anyone worth knowing and caring about."

Amanda didn't speak. She just looked at us. At all

of us. Then she took Suleiman out of the arena, back to his stall.

Uncle Bart watched her go. Then he swore, which he never does. And he swore again.

"What are you going to do?" Althea asked.

"What can I do? Refuse to work with the new rider, of course, if Girodani decides to change. Blast it, Althea, and the farm was going to turn a profit this year."

"It'll be all right."

"No, it won't. It won't be all right until things change. What Amanda says is true. Girodani doesn't think he's a bigot, but he is. He's making a big mistake, taking the girl off that horse. She's the only one who can handle him to a win."

"What's a bigot?" asked Denny.

"Not now, Denny," said Uncle Bart. "You kids run on up to the house. Darn it. Darn it! What a tragedy this is."

"What's a *bigot*!" Denny yelled. "I want to know what *a bigot* is, Natalie."

"Um," I said. "Well . . ."

"Bigots are people utterly intolerant of any person different from themselves," Althea said. "They are small shabby miserable people." Her tone was fierce. "Miserable."

Uncle Bart got his firm look. "Nat. Take Denny up to the house. It's getting on toward his bedtime."

Denny went with me without argument for once.

Outside, it was dark. The lights in the house were on, but the rest of the farm was cloaked in shadow. Above us the moon reflected white from the clouds, making the sky as bright as dawn. Denny walked alongside of me for a bit, not saying anything.

"Is Mr. Loomis really going to take Amanda out of the show, Natalie?"

"I guess so."

"Why?"

"Because her skin's a different color than his."

"Does that mean she can't ride good?"

"Rides well, Denny," I corrected. Honest, this kid's grammar was atrocious. "She rides like a dream. You saw her."

"I don't get it."

I didn't quite get it either, but I wasn't about to admit it to my dopey little brother. Denny tried again. He is what Dad calls persistent. Persistent is when a person like Denny keeps on nagging and nagging about the same thing. "If she was green, could she ride?"

"Don't be dopier than you already are, Dennis Carmichael Ross. Green isn't a human color."

"If she was white, could she ride?"

"Den—" I stopped right there in my tracks. Of course! If Amanda were white . . . I touched the pearl necklace. Still there. If the magic could make a stallion snooze right in the middle of a lighted arena filled with people—it sure as heck could turn Amanda white.

"Denny," I said. "I've got this great idea."

But did I? What made a person's skin the color it was? Denny could rearrange the molecules of things, but he couldn't add or subtract anything. And I kept thinking about the poem Althea had explained to me.

"Things fall apart . . . the center cannot hold." You couldn't mess with the basic nature of things—or it'd all fall apart. So I couldn't use the magic to change Amanda into a white person. But maybe I could just make Amanda's skin *look* white.

A cloud drifted across the moon, changing the white clouds to black in a moment.

White to black.

The cloud drifted away. The clouds turned white again.

Black to white.

Light! What if Denny could make Amanda's skin reflect light? Just like the moon turning the clouds to white.

Jeez!

There were footsteps on the graveled drive from the barn. Amanda's. I could tell that quick dancer's step anywhere. "Amanda!" I called. "Wait up." I grabbed Denny's hand and we ran toward her. I slowed down as we came up to her. Maybe I should think this through for a bit. I mean, how was I going to explain this? Like, "Yo!, Amanda, Denny and I can do this magic, see, with the help of a huge turtle."

Right. It would definitely be the funny farm for Natalie Ross.

Or, "Amanda. Hey. We can help you by turning you—just temporarily, you understand—well, turning you . . . white. Just close your eyes for a second. Don't worry, Denny and I can do this trick . . ."

"Hello, Natalie." She seemed just the same. Cool. Remote. She was standing very still in the moonlight. Wasn't she mad about Mr. Loomis? Wasn't she sad about losing the chance to ride Suleiman?

"Are you okay, Amanda?"

She sighed, very quietly. "I'll be fine." She moved away from us. "I can't stop to talk. I'm tired. I've got to call Mama and tell her what happened today and it's going to be a long long phone call. I'll leave you all now, okay?"

"Amanda. About tonight . . . in the arena . . ."

She whirled as if something finally snapped. Her body was tense, but her words were even. "What? What about tonight?" She moved closer. I could see her eyes glittering. "You want to tell me you're sorry about people like Jeff Loomis and his father? Do you? Do you want to tell me *you* don't think like that? No, not you. Not your uncle. Not any of you. Any of you." She sobbed, sudden like. "You can't know. You don't know. You *hear* that, girl?"

"We didn't do anything," Denny said.

I could see her take a deep breath. Swallow hard. Then she said, the calm back in her voice, "No, you didn't. Mama told me when this happens—you ignore it. Mama told me when they give you grief, you give them your back. You walk away. You walk away proud."

"You could walk away white," said Denny. This is one of the very few things that's good about being six. You can say very strange things and people will just laugh.

Amanda just laughed.

I tried to laugh like a grown-up: "Ha-ha." Then I said, "Actually, Denny's right. We do have this stuff.

It's just temporary"—I hoped—"and it will get you through the show tomorrow."

"To turn me *white*? No thanks. And then what?" There was a note in Amanda's voice I didn't understand. She sounded mad, not at me, at somebody else. Mr. Loomis, probably. She repeated what she'd said before. "I'm a white girl for a day, and then what?"

"I don't know," I said, because I didn't. "But at least you can have one more ride."

"One more ride," she said, with a sadness you could practically touch. "Shoot. This is ridiculous."

We were all quiet for a minute. Back in his stall, Suleiman whinnied, at Mindy Blue, maybe, because I heard her whinny back. Amanda lifted her head, listening. "It doesn't make any difference to them. At least I have that." She punched me lightly on the arm. "Thanks anyway, guys. I'll see you tomorrow, I guess." She walked away, the moonlight turning her skin to silver. "White!" I heard her say.

And she laughed.

# CHAPTER

## thirteen

THE NEXT DAY STILLMEADOW WAS A CRAZY PLACE. The trials at Uncle Bart's were only one of, like, twenty or thirty being held around the world that day. There are hundreds of riders who would sell their dog to even groom at a qualifying trial, much less ride in it. Everybody wants a shot at the Olympics. Uncle Bart had invited ten top riders who'd scored the highest points on the A-circuit that year to come. Special judges would be there to score the riders' performances.

The riders were coming in before breakfast. They were driving vans and pickup trucks and pulling horse rigs and trailers. Everybody was very very nervous. Even the horses. Uncle Bart says that horses pick up the personal vibrations of the people around them. Whenever he says psychic stuff like this, Mom rolls her eyes and goes, "Oh, Bart!" which reminds me of me, saying "Oh, Denny!" when Denny does something truly dumb. Uncle Bart is the smartest person I know about horses, except maybe John Ironheels, the barn manager. So I don't know why Mom does this except that she was never, like, even remotely horsey, and can't understand them. Anyhow, I had to get up really early to do morning chores. I didn't care. It was going to be an exciting day.

Mindy Blue was looking all around with her ears up when I went to her stall to get her after morning feed. There were a lot of strange horses in the barn, what with people coming from as far as New York City to be in the show. Mindy Blue seemed to want to say hi to every one of them.

I wished Mom wasn't in Paris, but right here, so that she could see how beautiful Mindy looked with her ears up and her eyes an eager brown. Mom would have changed her mind about being horsey, then.

Even though Mindy wasn't in the show, I brushed her until her chestnut coat shone. Then I braided her mane and tail. I made nice flat braids, right against her neck. I tied them with blue ribbon, because of her name. Then I turned her out in her day paddock with Susie, Denny's bratty little Shetland pony. Denny had tied a red ribbon around Susie's tail, which was pretty smart. A red ribbon around a horse's tail is not to look pretty, but to warn other riders that the horse might kick. Mindy Blue looked at that red ribbon, and snorted. Then she moved away from Susie to graze in the farthest corner of the paddock. Susie gave a little whinny like, "teehee," and galloped over to Mindy Blue. She looked like a toy rocking horse with her little short legs going up and down. She gave Mindy a bite in the rear. Mindy kicked out with one powerful hind leg. She missed Susie—on purpose, of course—but Susie could tell Mindy Blue meant business. Susie skipped away, going tee-hee again. But she didn't bother Mindy Blue again.

"I wish I could kick Jeff Loomis like that," I muttered. I tried it, pretending I was a horse and kicking backward with my right leg.

"Ow!"

I turned around. Jeff Loomis was hopping around on one leg. "Sorry," I said, not really meaning it, "but you should have warned me you were there." I started to walk away.

"Hey, wait up!"

I stopped. "First of all, I can't believe you'd show your face around here after what my uncle said to you last night. Second of all—never mind. Beat it. I'm busy."

"What do you mean, 'second of all'?"

I stopped again, and gave him my best glare. "You really want to know? I think you and your whole family stink."

"Oh, yeah?"

"Yeah." I marched off. That dorky Jeff tried to march off with me! "Will you cut it out? What do you want, anyway?"

"Why have you got such an attitude?" he complained.

"Me? *You're* the one with the attitude. Look at the way you're treating Amanda! Why do you hate her so much?"

He shrugged. "She's all right."

"Then why did you call her names? And why do you want to steal her horse?"

"I don't really want to take her horse. It's just . . ." He sort of trailed off.

I looked him full in the face. I don't know if being next to the pearl necklace all the time was doing this or not, but all of a sudden I knew something I hadn't known before. "You're scared of Suleiman, aren't you?"

Jeff curled his lip. He definitely did not look as cool as Sean Penn when he did this. "I'm not scared of that horse."

But he was, I could tell. So none of this made any sense. "Tell me, Jeff. If you don't want to ride the horse, and you think Amanda's all right, then why the heck are you giving her grief?"

"My father . . . he . . . well . . . He thinks I want to ride more than I do, I guess."

"Then just tell him," I said. I mean—this was really dopey. If Jeff didn't want the horse and Mr. Loomis was buying the horse just for him, the simplest thing in world would be for Jeff to *say* so, for Pete's sake. And if Jeff backed off, then maybe Mr. Girodani wouldn't be so worried about Amanda riding the stallion.

And Denny and I wouldn't have to figure out how to use the magic to make Amanda white. I wasn't all that sure that Amanda wanted to be white, even for one day.

"I can't."

"Why not?"

"He's not like your dad, Natalie. I can't talk to him. You just don't understand."

That was for sure. Then, all of a sudden, I did. Jeff was scared of his father! Even more scared than of Suleiman. I was amazed. I mean—how could a person be scared of their dad? Then I thought about Mr. Loomis and his piggy face. I suddenly felt very sorry for Jeff Loomis. I said, as soft as I could, "Have you ever tried to talk to him about it?"

But that was all I was going to get out of Jeff Loomis. He walked away with his usual swagger, like he was king of the universe. But now I knew better. He wasn't feeling like a king at all. He was feeling like a drip.

I didn't see Amanda in the next few hours. Plus, I was so busy helping to move the visiting horses into their stalls and showing people where the bathrooms were and mucking out the stalls of the Stillmeadow horses that I didn't have a minute to try and find her. I saw her mom and dad, though. Her mom was a big woman with a warm, happy face. I could tell she was proud. Her dad had frizzy gray hair and big spectacles. They were sitting by themselves near the turnout paddocks on some lawn chairs they'd brought. Just before ten o'clock, when the first rider was to go on, I went over to say hi.

"I'm Natalie Ross," I said. "Are you Amanda's mom and dad?"

Mrs. Saadiq nodded slowly. She smiled at me. "Amanda's told me all about you. And your horse, Mindy Blue. She said you're quite a good rider."

"She did?" I could feel my face. It was pink. My

face turns pink at the worst times, mostly when I'm happy and trying to be cool about it. I hate this. "Well, I think she's wonderful!"

"We do, too," said Mr. Saadiq. "We'd hoped for quite a career for her." His face looked sad. I couldn't stand it. It was a beautiful day. The sun was shining. Everyone was happy. And poor Mr. Saadiq was sad because Amanda was an African-American. I leaned forward. "Excuse me," I whispered. "I wasn't going to say anything, but I think you might be surprised at how well Amanda does today."

Mr. Saadiq raised his eyebrows. "I might?" he asked.

I nodded. "You might. You just wait and see."

The trumpet sounded to signal the start of the trials. Mr. and Mrs. Saadiq got up to go find Amanda. I patted my neck to make sure the pearl necklace was still there, and went to find Denny.

I'd figured it all out the night before. Denny's magic could only move molecules around. He couldn't change stuff. Plus—I wasn't about to, like, fiddle around changing a person's insides anyway. I mean, who knows what might happen.

What I figured was this. In health class, we'd learned that our bodies were ninety-eight percent liquid. I wanted Denny to put a one-molecule-thick veil of water on Amanda's skin. The lights in the arena and the light from the sun would reflect off this extra skin and turn her a silver color—just like the moon. Maybe Amanda would like being white so much that she'd want this water veil on her all the time. If she was white, people like Mr. Loomis and Jeff couldn't call her names. She wouldn't have to be better than everyone else to get somewhere in this life. She could just be a regular person if she wanted to.

I found Denny and Brandy out by the creek that runs through the big pasture, building the biggest mud pile I'd ever seen.

"Denny, you're filthy." I grabbed him by the T-shirt and dragged him out of the mud. Then I tried to scrub some of the mud off his face with the tail of my work shirt. It didn't help that Brandy was jumping around licking both of us. Pretty soon we were both muddier than heck and covered with dog spit.

The trumpet sounded the second call: the rides were about to begin.

"C'mon, Denny."

"Huh-uh. I want to finish this castle."

"That's not a castle. That's a toxic-waste dump. There's all kinds of goo in it." I picked up a stick and poked at it. "Yuck! There's even horse manure in there."

"It sticks good," Denny said.

There was his grammar again! "It doesn't stick good, it sticks well."

"Yep," said Denny. He was being agreeable. He squished to the other side of the little stream and started picking out rocks from the banks.

"We've got to go, Denny. The trials are starting."

"I don't care. I want to *finish this*!"

I knew that roar. I wasn't going to get anywhere with him. Now what was I going to do? It didn't do any good to grab him. With this magic, if you did it when you were angry or in a hateful mood—all that would happen is that beast would show up. If I'd learned anything about this magic in the last couple of days, it was that you had to do it in a nice way, with good thoughts all over the place. I stuck the not-so-good thought that Denny was a booger in the back of my mind. "I really need you now, Denny. Won't you come with me?"

"What for?"

"What for? What for?" Um. This was another problem. Denny didn't remember that he could do magic unless he was doing it. So if I said that I needed him to put a one-molecule-thick veil of water over Amanda Saadiq so she'd look like a white girl, he'd think I was nuts.

"Remember when we told Amanda last night that we could turn her white?"

"Nope." Denny waded through the stream and stuck a big piece of glop on top of his castle.

"Yes, you do."

"Well, kind of."

"I want to do it now. And I want you to help me."

"I can't do anything. And I don't want to watch the rides. It's boring. I'd watch the rides if I could ride Susie, but Uncle Bart says I can't. So I want to make my mud castle."

The starting signal for the second dressage rider floated though the air. I'd checked the board that morning; Amanda and Suleiman were scheduled back-to-back in the dressage competition and the stadium jumping; she was last to ride dressage and the first to jump. There were eight riders competing and the rides were about six minutes each—so I didn't have much time. I sloshed through the water to where Denny was decorating his mud castle with draggled old dandelions. I knelt down in the mud so I could look at him eyeball to eyeball. "Hey, Dennis."

"What."

"Help me. Please."

Well, the seriousness of it worked, which just goes to show you that six-year-olds have *some* clue about the world. He made a big deal of going with me, naturally, grumping along like a cranky person. But he came. And that was all I needed.

The best place to do the magic was behind the door of Uncle Bart's office. We could keep the door open a crack so the magic would get out, but keep ourselves concealed. And it was right near the entrance to the arena, where all the riders lined up, waiting to go in.

Amanda and Suleiman were circling in the drive, warming up. Mr. and Mrs. Saadiq stood by, looking proud but worried. The horse looked great. His coat was polished. His hooves shone. His mane was neatly braided and lay flat against his neck. Every single bit of his tack had been cleaned and oiled.

Amanda was astride him in her white breeches and black boots. Her black dressage coat was fitted closely to her. Her rider's number was tied around her middle: number forty-two. She looked glamorous; remote; like a star. At the same time I knew I had seen her in the same way before. Then it hit me. Yikes! I *had* seen her before. In the pearl sea! *She looked like the ebony girl on the silver horse!*

"That's it!" I whispered to Denny. "We are protecting the jewel, just like the turtle said. We *are* making a good use of the magic."

"Next entry! Number forty-two!" called Uncle Bart.

I peered around the edge of the door into the arena. The bleachers were filled with people. Except for the Loomises, Mr. Girodani, and all the Stillmeadow staff, I didn't recognize a single face. There were three judges, sitting behind a long table at the middle part of the arena.

I turned around. Amanda touched her heels lightly to Suleiman's sides. He pranced by, proud and happy.

I touched the necklace and drew it over my head. I folded Denny's hand in mine. The misty rose of the pearl sea rose around us. Denny's eyes reflected magic green.

"We need a veil of water, Denny," I whispered. "Very thin. Just one speck thin. All over Amanda's face and hands and neck. Any skin that shows. Okay?"

Amanda's special music, the music that she and the stallion rode to, sounded in the arena. The magic flew from Denny's fingers in a thin, steady stream. Water molecules whirled and whirled, a little waterfall. They met and paired: two molecules of hydrogen, one molecule of oxygen. Denny flung out his hands as if he were sowing wildflowers a handful at a time. The water spun and sparkled . . .

. . . and wrapped around Amanda. Just like Saran Wrap! It was so cool! Amanda didn't even feel it.

And even better . . .

It worked! The light reflected off her skin like the sun off the moon. Amanda became a white girl! She rode Suleiman into the arena and began the movements of fourth-level dressage, test one: shoulder in; half pass; reinback; canter serpentine with flying changes—

It was beautiful.

It was perfect.

It was the best ride I'd ever seen.

"What in *blazes* is going on!"

I jumped about a foot. I peered around the door. Mr. Saadiq was staring at his daughter. His face was . . .

Angry.

Furious.

I've never seen anyone madder in my whole entire life. And there was something even worse, if that were possible.

The magic was wrong. I felt the shadow of the beast. The unmistakable presence of that cold cold Thing.

"Denny," I said, "I think we made a mistake."

# CHAPTER

## fourteen

THEY HEARD ME, THE SAADIQS. MR. SAADIQ PULLED open the door and stood there frowning.

"Um, hi. Again," I said.

"Is this the surprise you were telling us about?" Mrs. Saadiq asked. Her tone was gentle. I think this was because she saw that I was scared of Mr. Saadiq's anger.

"Kind of. Yeah."

Mrs. Saadiq looked at her husband. There were no tears in her eyes, but the magic was in me and I could feel them. She was sad. She was more than sad. She was in terrible grief. She bent down so that her eyes were on a level with mine. "Natalie. You must tell me. Did Amanda want you to do this thing?"

"No, ma'am."

"How did you *do* it!" Mr. Saadiq said. He was still mad. But he was trying not to be. "How did you force my daughter to betray her race?"

Mrs. Saadiq saw I was confused, thank goodness. There is nothing worse than having an adult so totally mad at you they can hardly talk, they are so bummed out. "What Mr. Saadiq means by that, Natalie? That we are proud of being black. That we would not change ourselves for any reason on this earth. We've suffered, yes. Life is harder for us in some ways than for you, yes. But we are who we are. And it is a terrible thing to betray that. To deny it. Do you know who Judas Iscariot is? He is a man who betrayed his god. To do what Amanda has done is to betray her very self. And her father. And me."

"Oh, dear," I said. I mean, I couldn't think of a thing to say. "I'm sorry" was not going to hack it.

The signal sounded. Amanda's dressage ride was over. There was cheering and applause. A couple of adults came out of the arena. One was the woman who had agreed with Jeff Loomis when Kevin called Amanda the N-word. Her eyes swept briefly past the Saadiqs; she acted like they weren't even there. "That girl was simply stunning," she said to the man beside her. "Is she European, do you think? She had most unusual looks."

"Russian," said the man, like he knew, "Sadik is a Russian name. And those cheekbones and nose are Slavic."

"Very fine ride," said the woman. "If that stallion can jump, she should qualify for the team." They blathered on past us.

Then Amanda came out. She was riding in a daze. She'd pulled off one riding glove and was looking at her hand with this very strange expression. "Mama?" she said. "Daddy?"

"Get off that horse," said Mr. Saadiq in this tight voice. "And wash that stuff off. What *is* it, for heaven's sake?"

"I don't *know*," said Amanda. "Honestly, I don't know! I can't understand how this happened!"

"We did it," said Denny. All three of them turned and stared at me. I stole a look at Denny. The magic was in his eyes. Thank goodness no one else could see it! I dropped Denny's hand real fast, and stuck the necklace in my pocket.

"You did this, the two of you?" Mr. Saadiq said.

The bell sounded for the jumping class. Amanda gave a little cry, like, "Oh, no!"

"Well, we sort of fiddled with the lights in the arena, sir," I said. "And, um—we kind of put some powdery stuff on Amanda's clothes so that . . . so that . . ."

The buzzer sounded again. "Mama, I've got to go!" Amanda sounded frantic.

"Pull out of the class," Mr. Saadiq said sternly. "No daughter of mine is going to be dishonest."

"I'll fix the lights, sir," I said desperately. "Just let her ride, please. If she misses this ride, she forfeits the whole competition!"

"Clement," said Mrs. Saadiq, "if the girl can fix this . . ."

"Everyone will see," I promised. "It'll take just a few seconds. Truly."

"Miss Saadiq?" One of the judges came out of the arena entrance. "We're ready for you."

Amanda looked at her father. Her eyes were desperate. "Daddy? Please?"

Mr. Saadiq bent a very stern eye on me. "Young lady?"

"I'll fix it right now. Two seconds." I grabbed Denny and the two of us beat feet into Uncle Bart's office. As we scurried out of the way I heard Mrs. Saadiq begin to laugh. She laughed and laughed. "Daddy?" I heard her say to Mr. Saadiq. "Did you see that judge's face when that white girl called you Daddy? Daddy!"

"At least she's not mad anymore," said Denny. "Can I go back to the creek now?"

"Not just yet, Denny. We've got to get someplace where we can see Amanda ride."

"Natalie!" Uncle Bart charged into the office. He looked like—bewildered. "There's something very funny going on."

"I heard Mrs. Saadiq laugh," said Denny. "She thinks there's something funny going on, too."

"Not funny ha-ha, Denny. Funny peculiar. Amanda . . . I mean . . . she's . . ." He sort of flopped his hands around. His mouth opened and shut like a fish. Outside the office door, in the arena, I heard the sound of Suleiman galloping. He was starting to take the jumps.

"Denny and I are going to watch Amanda and Suleiman ride, Uncle Bart," I said.

"Watch Amanda. Right. Watch . . . Natalie, have you *seen* her?"

"Well, sure, Uncle Bart. Just now."

"Did you notice anything—anything . . ." He flapped his arms again.

"I think the lights are kind of funky," I said. "She looked a little, um—pale."

"Pale! Yes! The lights! Yes! The power company."

"I'm going to watch now, Uncle Bart."

He picked up the phone. Then he put it down again. "What the heck do I say to the power company?"

I twirled my hair around one finger and tried to look like I didn't know a thing. "Maybe the lights just need adjusting, or something."

He looked at me a little wild, like. Maybe it was because his hair was all which way from his pulling on it. "Adjusting. Yes. I'll get a ladder. You and Denny—if anyone asks . . . oh, never *mind*! Just go watch the show."

Uncle Bart disappeared to find a ladder, I guess. I grabbed Denny's hand. We went around the outside of the arena to find a place where we could see Amanda and work the magic again.

There was a little door on the other side that let the people from the bleachers go in and out without having to cross the entire arena to the big entrance. That would be a good place.

Denny and I slipped through the door and crawled under the stand. Suleiman and Amanda were flying around the arena in a thunder of hooves. The fences had been set at three feet six inches. Suleiman took them like a giant cat; easy, graceful, free.

I pulled the pearl necklace out of my pocket. As

soon as I had it in my hand, I knew we had to fix what we'd done to Amanda.

Because the beast was there, waiting.

I could feel it even before I grabbed Denny's hand to start the magic. I heard the icy whisper—**dennydennydenny**—and I was *truly* petrified. I held Denny close to me. Just before I took his hand, I said. "If something calls you—you don't answer, right?"

"Huh?"

"Just trust me, Dennis Ross. If anyone, any *thing* calls you, you stay right here. With me. And you *do not* let go of my hand. Ever. You got that?"

Denny shrugged.

"I mean it, Denny. On my life."

"*Okay.*"

I took his hand in mine. It was gritty with the mud from the creek. And horse manure, probably. "You disassemble the water, Denny. Take it away from her skin."

As soon as the green fire sprang from Denny's hands, I knew things were terribly wrong. The green fire from Denny's fingers was a pale and sickly thing. The little specks, the molecules, spun faster and wilder, out of control. The specks flew in all directions.

*Chaos,* said the Voice of the Turtle.

The nearness of the Thing increased. The cold cold sound of its whispered call swept over Amanda's music. I knew, I *knew* that if the beast's voice drowned out the music of Amanda's ride, that Thing would get closer than ever.

So I started to sing. The song of the spell:

"All magic is linked
By heart and mind.
What's white is black;
Black's white in kind."

And the turtle sang with me..

*The hearts of good things are the same.*
*You'll find*
*Your center yourself if you leave hate behind.*

The beast drew back, I could feel it. We sang it again, the turtle and I, and again.

And the Thing finally left us alone.

"Now, Denny," I said.

This time the green fire from his hands was as fresh as spring. The little specks whirled and the water molecules flew away. Amanda and Suleiman thundered down the center of the arena, headed for the final jump. The magic whirled, sparkled. . . .

Suleiman gathered himself for the final, powerful leap. The magic shone around them both . . .

. . . and Amanda was her ebony self again.

The crowd gasped. Suleiman leaped. He arched over the jump with a mighty spring, and landed, soft as a cat.

Amanda turned him and rode back through the center of the arena. The crowd was absolutely silent. Stone-cold quiet. I wondered if the beast had well and truly gone.

Amanda's head was high and proud. The lights glanced off her dark dark skin. The lights flickered. Uncle Bart was fooling with them. They went out.

Came back on again to reveal Amanda and the stallion, black against white, white against black, as beautiful as the sun in the morning.

"Just a little problem with the lights, folks!" boomed Uncle Bart over the sound system. "I hope we can all see her clearly now. Stillmeadow Farms is proud to present our first champion to qualify for the next round to the Olympics, Amanda Saadiq!"

I dropped Denny's hand. I started to clap. Denny went "Yayyy!"

And the crowd cheered, too.

I hung around the arena until the shouting died down and Amanda took Suleiman back to his stall to tack down and cool out. I wasn't exactly sure what I was going to say to her. So I didn't say anything at all. I just sort of walked up and stood there as she unbuckled Suleiman's girth and removed the saddle.

"I'll put the saddle away," I said.

She didn't look at me. "I've got it. Thanks."

"Want me to bring the sponge and bucket?"

She shook her head. She clipped Suleiman into the cross ties. I picked up the body brush and began to wipe down Suleiman's flank. Amanda eased it out of my hand. "I'll take care of this," she said. "You go on. I think your uncle may need you."

"Are you really mad at me?"

She stepped away from the horse. "Yes. I'm really angry."

"I'm sorry. I only wanted to help."

"You only wanted to erase me, you mean. You only wanted to show everyone in that entire arena that I was a piece of trash."

Her voice was even. Terrible words were coming out of her, and her voice was, like, totally controlled. They were terrible words I deserved, I guess.

"You're the best rider Uncle Bart's ever had at the farm. I only wanted people to see that. I didn't want—"

Her voice was still even, but her hands were shaking. "You wanted to take away my soul. You wanted me, Amanda, not to exist. My color is as much a part of me as my love for this horse."

Suleiman tossed his head and snorted. Even he was mad at me.

So we weren't a team anymore. I walked out of the barn, feeling pretty bad, and walked straight into Althea. She'd been standing watching all the rigs loading up and leaving Stillmeadow.

"Sorry," I said.

"You look pretty sorry," she said. "Natalie, were you responsible for that craziness?"

"Sort of."

"When I told you that sometimes you have to take action—I didn't mean that you . . ." She trailed off. "Well, that you should do what you did."

"Amanda won't talk to me."

"I'm not surprised. That was an awful insult."

Dumb old tears prickled my eyes. Althea gave me sort of an exasperated hug. "She may forgive you. Just give her a little time. She's a great person and I've never known her to hold a grudge. But then, she may not." She got a funny look on her face. "You know, Natalie, people can make a career of doing good, you know what I mean? And they do good things because it makes them feel good, as if they are better than everyone else. You're going to have to learn a little humility, honey."

So I wasn't helping Amanda? I was just making myself feel good? That I wasn't thinking of who she really was?

Suleiman's voice echoed in my head: "She is what she is, my dear. And she is the best at what she is."

This was true. So Amanda and I might be friends again, as long as I got Suleiman's message through my thick skull. We might even be a team again. Just as long as I stood up for Amanda as herself, and not somebody else.

This was one thing I'd have to learn with this damn magic: that the beast could hide in good feelings, and wasn't just obvious with the bad ones like hate and meanness. I was, like, totally bummed. I'd believed the wrong thing and misunderstood the real message—that one is all and all are one. I'd screwed everything up.

"Natalie?" said Althea in a gentle way. "What's wrong?"

"But we're the same," I said. "Aren't we? Amanda and I are just the same."

"Of course you are. It's a basic truth that each of us is all of us, but all of us are individuals. A great truth. That everyone needs to know." She got a funny look on her face. "And in a way, Natalie, what you did today was show everyone that this is true. Amanda's ride had nothing to do with her color. And everyone saw it. So maybe it wasn't all bad, what you did. Tough on you, of course. I'm sorry."

I thought about this for a second. I should have known. This magic wasn't going to be easy. I was going to have to be tough to use it. I was going to have to, like, stand up for it, like Althea said.

Jeez!

The rest of the day was pretty busy, so Denny and I didn't get to do any more magic. Which was okay by me. I was, like, totally pooped, and ready for a good night's sleep. I slept really hard. I dreamed of the turtle and what he might bring.

Mary Stanton lives on a horse farm in upstate New York with some of the horses featured in the stories about Natalie and Denny. Her first two novels, *The Heavenly Horse of the Outermost West* and *Piper at the Gates of Dawn*, are about horses, too.

Mary writes adult mysteries as Claudia Bishop. She also writes for television.